A Woman's
Strident Voice Sounded
Somewhere Above Him.

He got up and crouched on the marble stoop to peer over the edge of the grave. Once again, baby pink; the long arm of the law had arrived. Yet another woman clad in the familiar pink garment stood a short distance away with her back to him, scolding the zombie crew clustered about the working grave.

Owen knew her problem. She had heard him talking, she had overheard him trying to strike up a conversation with the crew while she was lollygagging in the timber, or whatever she was doing in there, and had come out to learn the reason. Talking wasn't permitted among the males.

Owen waited until she ran out of breath. He stood up straight on the marble stoop with his head and shoulders aboveground.

"Hi, there, cupcake! I'm grave-robbing."

The woman spun around in startled disbelief.

Owen looked at her ashen face and then her crumpling body as it tumbled into the weedy grass.

"Now, ain't that just like a woman?" he asked the zombies. "Give them a straight answer and they faint dead away."

RESURRECTION DAYS

DAYS

WILSON TUCKER

A TIMESCAPE BOOK
PUBLISHED BY POCKET BOOKS NEW YORK

Another *Original* publication of TIMESCAPE BOOKS

A Timescape Book published by
POCKET BOOKS, a Simon & Schuster division of
GULF & WESTERN CORPORATION
1230 Avenue of the Americas, New York, N.Y. 10020

ISBN: 0-671-83242-5

First Timescape Books printing November, 1981

10 9 8 7 6 5 4 3 2 1

POCKET and colophon are trademarks of Simon & Schuster.

Use of the TIMESCAPE trademark under exclusive license
from trademark owner.

Printed in the U.S.A.

For Ralph and Phyllis,
who waited with patience.

W.T.

One

'Tis the voice of the sluggard; I heard him complain; "You have waked me too soon, I must slumber again."

—Isaac Watts

Owen Hall's first day of his new life began with uncertainty, misdoubt. It was a second life, his second time around, and that contributed to the confusion. His very first look at this new world convinced him it was not the promised land, not the Eden-like garden he had been led to expect. Someone had robbed him of that.

He had been thwacked on his bottom and shoved, rudely. They weren't supposed to do that in Utopia.

Owen Hall was a reborn but troubled man.

In that first moment of total awareness, of knowing he was alive again, Owen found himself standing outside a door and facing a road that moved. The road flowed slowly eastward toward a rising sun, a road wholly without bumps, potholes, mile markers, or the familiar yellow line down the middle to guide irresolute travelers. Owen stared at the moving road and thought the new world a very odd place. It was definitely *not* what the pastor had promised him.

He craned his head around to look at the door behind him. It was painted a sickly green and bore a number that meant nothing—it wasn't *his* house number.

That door had been slammed shut behind him after he was so rudely pushed through it, although there was no distinct recollection of his passage through the doorway or who had done the shoving. It was reasonable to assume that the same person was responsible for both acts. He'd felt a powerful thrust across the small of his back, an equally powerful thwack across his bottom, and he had been propelled from a darkened interior out into the brilliant light of a new day. The same heavy hand had then slammed the door behind him, and here he was: Owen Hall, alive in a new world. Awareness of self and awareness of his surroundings began with that discourteous ejection.

Owen Hall thought it a damned poor way to send a guest down the road.

The new sun hurt his eyes because he'd been used to a long darkness. It was rising with the quick heat of summer, rising into a cloudless sky that surely promised hot and discomforting hours to come. He thought it was a July or an August sun, but it *shouldn't* be summertime.

A July or an August sun was out of place, as strange as that flowing roadway. *This* should be late winter. There *should* be ice and snow on the land. He found a fleeting memory of snow everywhere, of ice on a highway, of a blizzard around him and stinging his face. He should be in the middle of winter, not in the early morning of a hot summer day. Not only had the pastor misled him, somebody had turned the seasons around when he wasn't looking.

"I've been had," he muttered aloud.

There was a healthy stand of summer grass on either side of the walk where he stood, and an enormous prairie of grass just over there beyond the rolling road. That prairie seemed to fill all of the new world from one horizon to the other, occupying all of the visible world across the roadway. The lush turf was everywhere, as the pastures and the croplands had once been everywhere before the subdivisions came. This was clean, green country unspoiled by highways, billboards, and hamburger houses, much the same as it had been in his youth—open country where a boy or a man could roam to his heart's content. That one part of the world could be the promised land.

In the far distance—off there to the east—a stand of timber grew against the horizon, fine trees standing tall before the sun. Now that was good. The day was already so bright that he had to squint to see the timber. Owen thought he just might go over there and see that timber—it would be cool there when the day grew unbearably hot, and he could sit a batch and try to puzzle out this business. A headful of blackness where his memory should have been really irritated him.

The road again claimed his attention. It moved.

The flowing roadway was actually a street, now that he examined it closely—a wide and smoothly surfaced street that flowed toward the rising sun at a speed equal to a fast walk. It rolled in from the southwest in a gentle arc, coming from someplace beyond his sight, and curved gently around an endless row of low buildings as it approached him. The road served the row houses from southwest to northeast, following the building line.

All of the buildings were identical to the one he'd been thrown out of, with one small exception. They had plain fronts, were one-story high, and were without windows; the houses abutted one another as if to prop each other up, and each had a small plot of grass in front with a narrow walk leading to the roadway. The door to each house was painted a different color, the only distinguishing mark other than the numbers.

Owen Hall inspected the street and the town with a growing sense of wonder. He guessed that it was a round town, a self-contained ring, and that the moving street completely encircled it in an endless loop. A small pinprick of memory helped him make that guess; there had been something about the concept in one of the science wonder magazines, some prophecy of the amazing things to come in a technological future. The roads must roll to replace the automobile.

There was no telling what science would do next.

In the next moment that mysterious green door behind him was yanked open and a woman shouted belligerently—shouted at him.

"Hey, you, dummy!"

Owen turned around to examine this newest wonder. He was quickly astonished at sight of her.

The woman popped through the door and nearly lost her balance, but managed to shake a balled fist at him.

"What are you doing there, dummy?"

Owen took a prudent step backward.

The woman was an ogre. She was about forty years old and distinctly chunky through the middle parts; her arms and legs were uncommonly thick—solid—and her huge hands were obviously capable of hurling him through any number of doorways. He realized at once those hands *had* thrown him through *that* doorway.

"Good morning, ma'am."

The woman came on, following him down the walk. Her hair was black, her eyes were angry, and her height was impressive—she towered at least six inches above him, looming over him like a tall tree in a strong wind.

The ogre was clad from neck to sandals in tight, form-fitting pink clothing. Baby pink. The single garment resembled a mechanic's overalls, and it might have been flattering if it were not for that unsightly bulge around the middle, if it were not for her elephantine weight. She staggered as she approached him.

"I *asked* you, dummy, what're you doing here? *What?*"

Her voice was a hoarse bellow and the wind that blew from her mouth was freighted with an old familiar smell. Owen recognized the odor of sour mash whiskey.

She belched in his face. "*Told* you to go to work! Now, *go.*" Again the rank breath washed down over him, falling on him from her greater height. "Go on, dummy!"

Owen was impressed. "Honey, you're loaded."

Ignoring the accusation or perhaps not understanding it, the belligerent woman stumbled closer and bent to peer into his eyes. He was splashed with the eighty-six proof gale winds and made ready to jump aside if she came tumbling down on him. His new life would be a very short one if she pinned him to the ground.

"Easy, now—go easy."

"What's wrong with you, dummy? What went *wrong?* How's your equilibrium? Huh?"

"There's nothing wrong with *my* equilibrium," Owen retorted. "Why did you shove me through that door? Why did you hit me behind? What's the big idea in all that?"

She peered down at him. "Can you walk without falling down? Now, huh?"

"I might ask you the same thing."

Owen discovered that he possessed a baritone voice and was quickly pleased. It had been a very long time since he'd listened to the sound of his own voice.

Another bellow. "There's something wrong with you!"

"Pot calling the kettle black," Owen retorted.

"Something went *wrong* in the mix, dummy."

"It smells that way," he agreed. "You didn't let it age long enough."

"I could *do* you over again."

Owen studied her bulk. "You can't run that fast."

A balled fist was held before his face. "The others don't talk back, dummy!"

"I do. I talk when I please. I'm a New Deal Democrat, and President Roosevelt gave us the Four Freedoms. Freedom of speech is one of them, and I talk to anybody." He studied her looming bulk. "Even you."

She jabbed him with a heavy index finger and it felt like an awl digging into his shoulder blade.

"Wrong, wrong, wrong, *wrong!*"

"Honey, your needle is stuck."

Owen backed away from the jabbing finger and the alcoholic wash. The ogre teetered precariously and was near falling. He realized the pushy, loud-mouthed woman wasn't his wife and was pleased again. The realization was a relief. Now that he thought about it, he knew he didn't have a wife—not here, not back there, nor anywhere. He had never married. A large and all-enveloping blackness still lived in his skull, displacing the memory that should have been there, but these stray remembrances that came through from time to time were most welcome. They were mere threads of his memory, but he clutched at them, saved them. The harridan wasn't his wife.

And again he wondered what he was doing in the new world, doing in *that* house, on *this* walk, arguing with a drunken behemoth. Why was he in her company at all? Most definitely, this was not the happy kingdom promised by the preachers—although it could be a version of the fiery pit they threatened for backsliders. That gauzy golden land in the sky wasn't likely to have drab row houses, moving roads predicted by technical magazines, and overweight females loaded to the eyeballs on homemade sour mash whiskey. *This* was something else altogether, but he didn't think the lurching lady was apt to explain it to him. Her mood was foul.

"Show me you can walk, dummy."

Owen obediently marched back and forth along the walk between the green door and the edge of the street.

His legs were strangely weak and for a brief moment he felt like an infant learning its first steps, but the uneasy feeling passed, and soon he was ambling along in his old rangy stride. Another stray remembrance, a wisp of his missing memory—his old rangy stride. He *knew* he was doing it right, knew he was walking in an old and familiar pattern, but he couldn't pin down just how he knew it was right. Perhaps his memory *was* returning, perhaps he would soon regain all his old skills. He had skills, of course—the skills he had learned back there in first life.

"How does it feel?" the woman demanded.

"Nothing to it. I walk all the time."

"You talk all the time, too."

"I have a natural wit."

"You ready to go to work?"

"Work?" Owen stopped pacing to ponder that and stared up into her face. "Well, now, I hadn't considered *working*. I thought I might mosey over to the timber, there, or maybe knock around the town to see what is going on here." He inched away from the secondhand whiskey. "What *is* going on here?"

"You go to work!" was the answering blast. "That's what you're *for*." And she seemed ready to topple again.

"Females always take that attitude," Owen said. "Why don't *you* go to work and let me go fishing?"

"Shut up, dummy. *Work!*" The very heavy fist was pushed up to his nose and waggled suggestively. The other hand was reaching for his shoulder but having trouble in finding it. "I can *do* you over again."

Owen jumped away, thoroughly alarmed. One of those heavy hands had smacked him across the rump and helped him through a doorway only a short while ago, and he didn't welcome another demonstration of strength now—nor did he care to go back indoors with the harridan.

"Work it is, honey. Yessiree, ma'am! I don't really mind if I do. It's the patriotic thing to do—did you know that? President Roosevelt said that honest work will help the country through these trying times—work will turn the lights on again in Europe. We've got to win the war." He watched the hands with a wary eye. "What work? Where? I can saw wood."

"The road, you dummy, get on the road." Sour mash fumes enveloped him. "That's what it's *for*. Follow those other dummies, go where they go. Work!" She waved both large arms with disgust. *"Mother,* are you *wrong."*

"I wouldn't want to be your mother. I don't even want to be your father. I'd go shoot myself."

"Get out there on the road with those other dummies and go to *work.* Stop talking!"

Owen craned around to look again at the rolling road and discovered it thinly populated. He revealed surprise. The road had been empty when he was demonstrating how to walk—at least, he hadn't seen anyone on it—but now men were beginning to appear. They were coming from the southwest, from those far distances down the road, riding toward him and past him to some unseen destination in the northeast. Going to work, wherever that was.

The men behaved like sleepwalkers, or dummies; they displayed all the energy and vitality of anemic zombies. They traveled singly, or in pairs, but there was no fraternization between them, no gossiping or retelling old ball scores—no one talked of Rogers Hornsby finally making the Hall of Fame after more than twenty-two hundred games and a batting average of .358; no one of them spoke to his fellow even though the fellow was alongside, elbow to elbow, cheek by jowl; no one cracked jokes about Betty or the other Bette. The workmen were models of inert bodies.

They didn't look up at Owen as they passed him, nor glance at his besotted companion; instead, they contented themselves with studying their shoes or the smooth roadway beneath their shoes, each carefully keeping his own quiet company. Now and again there was a rare individual who had forgotten to bend his neck and who spent *his* travel time absently contemplating the nape of the neck of the man standing next in front, but such men were few. A man emerged from a yellow door in the adjoining house and swung onto the roadway.

"What's wrong with all those guys?" Owen demanded. "They look like zombies, walking zombies."

There was no answer.

Owen turned around to question the woman, but she had left him. He watched her stagger up the walk toward the door. She collided with the doorframe, bounced off it, bellowed some unknown word in hurt or in frustration, and straightened for another attempt. The body gathered speed. Owen held his breath. The woman lumbered through the doorway and shouted again, hurling a command back to him. The command sounded like "Go, dum!"

The door was slammed shut.

Owen went.

Two

It's well to be off with the Old Woman before you're on with the New.

—George Bernard Shaw

He couldn't just stand there beside the road all day, gawking at technological marvels.

Owen Hall put away his indecision and stepped onto the moving belt. It very nearly threw him and he promptly jumped off again to examine the tricky thing. Technique and expertise were lacking, although once he *had* ridden a moving stairway in a St. Louis department store.

That boarding maneuver certainly wasn't familiar; he'd not done anything like that before. Owen got aboard a second time, swinging on awkwardly and again nearly losing his balance despite his being prepared for the forward motion. He braced his feet apart and teetered, noting with a small envy that the other riders weren't having his troubles. Well, maybe he could do better tomorrow, unless he skipped the whole nonsense to go fishing. It was more fun to fish than to work anyway.

Owen concentrated on the task for minutes, getting accustomed to the motion and learning how to maintain his balance. The soles of his feet detected an indefinable humming or whirring feel, to suggest that motors and wheels were spinning beneath the street. When he was satisfied that he could take his eyes off the road and his attention away from his feet without falling down, he looked about at his surroundings.

Row houses were flowing monotonously by him on the one hand and the great green prairie on the other. He preferred the prairie and gave it all of his attention, watching with keen expectation for a stream, a pond, or perhaps a gravel pit—almost any kind of water hole that promised a spot for fishing. Tomorrow *would* be a fine day for fishing. That sport was infinitely better than going to work, and President Roosevelt surely wouldn't mind him taking off just one day for relaxation. Even the President went for a restful cruise on the Potomac now and then.

Two objects on the prairie claimed his attention.

The first was an old cemetery. It was more than old, it was *ancient*—a place long abandoned by the looks of it. The marble monuments and the smaller stones had tumbled over in neglect, fallen to the vandals of time and wind, while weeds and tall grasses grew everywhere in an eager attempt to obliterate the remaining traces of the stones. Bases and pedestals were already lost to the weeds, and their presence had to be guessed at. Owen didn't think it likely the cemetery would offer any good fishing spots.

He was surprised to see some of the workmen ahead of him quit the road and plod along a path through the weeds toward the ancient graveyard. Owen stared open-mouthed. The workmen carried no spades, no tools of any kind that were visible to him, but the cemetery was their obvious destination. Six or eight men plodded along in single file through the entangling weeds, obediently following a zombie leader who seemed to know where he was going. Why work in an old cemetery?

Owen said aloud, "Rum bunch," and turned his gaze to the second attraction—to the timber he'd seen when he first examined the new world.

It was a magnificent stand of timber already in the full leaf of summer and it wheeled toward him in a kind of majestic splendor as the road carried him northeast. The place was inviting. It would be pleasantly cool under those trees, cool and inviting later in the day when the sun scorched the town. A place for introspection. Owen craned his head to watch as the timber wheeled past him, searching for birds or sign of small game within it. He made up his mind to investigate that cool place as soon as he had the free time, to stroll through it and see what could be found. Next to fishing, the woods were the best place for thinking and dreaming, the place for living yesterday over again and for plotting tomorrow before it came. With some luck, some prodding, he might even rediscover his memory there—*all* of his memory instead of the bits and pieces he now owned.

Yes, indeed, he'd certainly explore those woods.

The prairie seemed empty of other life: there were no cattle, no livestock of any kind, and nary a sign of a plow. The sod of that prairie had not been turned in a very long time—not for a small eternity, to judge by the overgrowth. Owen wondered if he was seeing buffalo grass. His grandfather had told him that the prairies were once covered by buffalo grass, before the sodbusters cut it up with plows or burned it off to make room for settlements. It would be a welcome sight to see one, just *one* farmhouse somewhere out there on the prairie—and preferably a farmhouse with a working windmill. A pleasurable sight.

The road carried him around the rim of the town. It reminded him of riding around the rim of the world.

There was nothing on the inside of the road but an unbroken row of drab houses and painted doors, buildings that were monotonously stacked side by side and holding each other up in mutual support. The houses clung together to demonstrate that misery loved company, while the many colored doors did little to improve their lot.

Men—zombie men—came out of countless doorways to join those others already riding the road—men plodded out of numerous warrens to take their wooden places alongside other wooden men—but none of them shouted hello or grumbled about the night before or told a dirty joke. No one knocked the St. Louis Browns or predicted when they'd climb out of the cellar. The men did nothing more than swing aboard the road with practiced step and then stand as if dead, waiting for whatever would happen next.

Owen Hall thought that was pretty stupid. He walked gingerly across the road and stared into the face of a newcomer.

"What's the name of this here town, sport?"

The fellow returned his stare for a fraction of a second, for no more than a tic in time, and then dropped his gaze to study his own feet.

Owen bent down, craned his neck against the man's chest, and peered up into the blockish face.

"Do you think the Senators will *ever* win the pennant?"

The fellow turned around to avoid him.

Owen told him aloud that was a hell of a thing for a grown man to do, and lost interest in the clod. Walking carefully because he had not yet mastered the technique of maintaining an easy balance on the roadway, he went forward a few paces and tapped another rider on the shoulder.

"Where can a thirsty man get a beer around here?"

The rider closed his eyes and hung his head.

"Well, then, where's a horse parlor?" Owen asked. "Where can a sporting man put down a few bucks?"

There was no response.

"Don't you even have a pool hall? Show me a pool hall and I'll show you where beer can be had."

No answer.

Owen said, *"You're* a live one! I'll bet you're a bushel of laughs at home."

He wandered back and forth along the road, staring impudently into unresponsive faces and asking questions —sensible and foolish questions to gain attention. There were no responding answers—sensible or foolish. He slid in between a pair of workmen who seemed to be traveling together, but was ignored by both of them. He plucked at a few elbows, accidentally stepped on somebody's toes, and gently rapped on one bald pate to provoke a reply, but his only reward after several minutes of experimentation was a long loud silence. His co-riders would not respond in any way or acknowledge his presence, except to turn away when he thrust his face against theirs. He was shirked, ignored, and cold-shouldered.

Owen told them loudly that they acted like a pack of zombies. He pronounced them dead around the ears. He said that if they fell down they'd be buried.

The zombies accepted his judgment without comment.

Owen's curiosity returned to the road itself. Now *there* was something alive, vibrant, and productive. The street hummed beneath his feet and he fancied that he could actually feel the powerful motors carrying out their only duty. Could those motors be seen, he wondered? Were the wheels visible? The mechanism was worth investigating.

Moving cautiously to the very edge of the rolling surface and taking care not to topple off into the grass, he dropped to his knees and looked over the side in search of a crack or seam in the construction materials, seeking a space between the road itself and whatever solid bed it rested on. There was nothing—no separating space.

Owen thought that failed to make sense; there *had* to be a crack, however thin, between the two bodies. If the road was suspended on jets of air, there ought to be little wheels somewhere inside to provide a forward motion; if mighty motors drove the thoroughfare, there should be larger wheels and gears and belts and things to speed it along; or if some new and unimaginable invention drove the road, that invention should be visible to his inspection. And, of course, there should be a nameplate or a patent plate attached to the side of the road giving the inventor due credit for his predictive engineering. That in turn would provide a patent number and a patent date.

He found nothing.

Owen was kneeling there, puzzling the matter, when someone tapped him on the shoulder. The finger had the feel of authority. A side glance revealed a pair of legs clad in pink coveralls—baby pink. Owen sighed, not really wanting to face that ogre again.

He said, "Hi, Mother. Did you bring the jug?"

"Stand up."

Owen obediently stood up and realized his mistake. *This* woman was not the ogre. *This* woman was dressed in the same fashion, in a similar garment, but most decidedly she was not the same female he had last seen stumbling and bouncing through a green doorway. This one had no bulge about the middle. This one was a few inches taller than the first and was several years younger; this one had sandy blonde hair, a slim figure, graceful hands, properly proportioned arms and legs, and a minute brown spot on the tip of her nose that might have been a freckle. A new woman.

This woman didn't bellow. She asked reasonably enough, "What were you doing down there?"

"Looking for the little wheels," Owen responded.

"What little wheels?"

"The little wheels this road runs on. They've got to be under there somewhere."

"Did you find them?"

"Nope."

"*Should* there be little wheels under it?"

"Well, yes—unless it runs on rubber bands."

"How do you know that?"

"I subscribe to *Amazing Mechanics* magazine."

The new woman peered closely at his eyes, bending down to study the pupils. Her extraordinary height was a bit unsettling, but he didn't think *she* would topple over. The newcomer was in complete control of her faculties.

She asked, "Are you well? Do you feel all right?"

"Of course I do. Want to dance?"

"Is your equilibrium satisfactory?"

"Now *there* it goes again!" Owen felt frustrated. "Why do you people keep asking that? There's nothing wrong with me—except that I don't remember last night. I don't remember much of me."

The pink young woman studied him in speculation. "Are you new?"

"New what? This town is a new one on me."

"What is a jug?"

"Booze, of course."

"What is booze?"

"The stuff that comes in a jug. You drink it." Owen decided the little freckle on the tip of her nose was fascinating. "I mean, you drink it when you can get it."

"Why?"

Owen said with some exasperation, "Oh, fudge! Go ask your sister."

"I have no sister. Where did you originate?"

"I don't know—back there somewhere." He waved a careless hand to indicate some vague distance behind and almost struck a man standing nearby. The workman blinked at his passing hand but didn't move away from them.

Owen turned on the waiting woman and said dryly, "Here, watch this." He deliberately thrust his index finger against the man's nose and pushed it off center. "Beep."

The man turned his back.

"See that?" Owen demanded. "No guts."

"Why did you do that?"

"For the hell of it. We need a little excitement around here. The town's pretty dead—haven't you noticed?"

She bent again to study his eyes. "Your behavior is most unusual. I suspect you are incomplete. Are you sure you don't remember your point of origin?" The woman watched his pupils for a reaction.

"Honey, I wouldn't go back there again if I *did* remember. That old bat was loaded, but she wouldn't share it—nary a drop." Owen looked at the back of the man standing nearby and suspected the fellow of eavesdropping. Nosy zombie. He grasped the young woman's hand and pulled her to the middle of the roadway, well away from the man. She seemed reluctant to move and he had to tug.

"Now we can talk," he explained. "These guys give me the creeps."

The woman in pink was startled by his action. "You touched me!"

Owen looked at her chest. "Want an encore?"

"No. Laborers do not touch wardens."

"I'll touch anybody," Owen said. "I'm broad-minded."

The woman did something that startled him in turn. Reaching for the flap on the breast pocket of his coveralls, she pushed her fingers down inside, rummaging about for something that she thought should be there. Owen looked down, following her fingers, and discovered for the first time that he was wearing dun-colored coveralls. Until now he just hadn't paid attention to what he was wearing. His garment wasn't as well tailored as hers, wasn't as neat and trim and form-fitting, but clearly it had come from the same manufacturer. All the men on the street were dressed alike, dressed as he was—a colorless pack of nobodies.

Owen asked, "What are you looking for—lint?"

The woman didn't answer but continued the search through the remaining pockets of the garment. All of them were empty. Pulling the loose collar away from his neck, she fingered the neckband all the way around without finding anything and then moved her search down the sleeves. Owen received a thorough frisking but nothing was found. The next maneuver unsettled him. The woman in pink didn't hesitate or offer an apology as she dropped to one knee before him and completed the frisk, running exploratory hands up and down the legs of his coveralls, inside and out. Owen looked on with embarrassment and no little amazement; he thought he might giggle if she kept on—he was ticklish *there*.

Discovery: a small oblong bar resembling stainless steel was found pinned to the cuff inside a trouser leg.

"Jackpot!" he cried. "What is it?"

"Your identification."

The warden removed the bar from the trouser cuff with an exclamation of annoyance and pinned it in the proper place under the flap of that breast pocket she had first searched. Owen watched as she placed the flat of her thumb on the bar and gently pressed it against his chest.

For the sheer fun of it, he did the same to her.

The young woman was taken aback by his gesture, almost shocked, but she stood her ground when she realized what he was doing. Owen rather liked what he was doing. An identical bar of steel was pinned beneath the flap of her breast pocket and it sank softly inward as he pushed.

A sensation was transmitted through his thumb—a peculiar feeling he didn't immediately recognize.

Owen lifted his thumb, looked at the underside of it with wonder, and returned it to the yielding steel bar. The sensation came again, and this time he realized what was happening. He was reading an identification. His thumb felt and read numbers imprinted on the bar—he was actually thumb-reading a message implanted there.

LH-350350-b08-136

"That is enough," she said, and removed his hand from her breast.

Owen put a thumb to his own pocket bar.

Recla/H-260702-30?

"Hey!" he cried in surprise. "Dig that crazy bug number. What's the question mark for?"

"Your original age is uncertain."

"No it isn't. I'm twenty-eight."

The woman zeroed in on that. "How do you know?"

"Well, I guess I ought to know my own age. I'm draft bait, I'm 1-A. The war and all, see?" His thumb went back to the identification bar for a second read. "What does *Recla/H* mean?"

She ignored the question. "Were you given direct instructions when you began this morning?"

"Began what?"

"When you left a house and mounted the road."

"Sure—I was told to follow these creeps to work."

"What else?"

"Nothing else—and here I am following these creeps to work." Owen looked around at his fellow passengers. "They're a sorry lot. Dead from the neck up."

"Were you given anything?"

"Hah! I was given a lot of bull from a drunken old broad. Honey, *she* was loaded."

The new woman betrayed her impatience. "Was there nothing more? Weren't you instructed to return to the house after finishing your work?"

"Nope—nothing like that."

"You don't recall your point of origin? What was the number on the door?"

"I don't know the number. It was a green door."

"There are hundreds of green doors. Do you remember the woman at the house?"

Owen shuddered. "I remember she was loaded."

"Loaded? She was weighted down? A burden?"

"She was loaded with booze. I mean, *looped.*"

"I don't know. What is looped? What is booze? Where did she obtain the looped booze?"

"How should I know?" Owen was quickly irritated. "Maybe she had a still in there, behind the green door."

"A still what?"

"Baby doll, you are one dull cat. Don't you know anything? Don't you know how to get on in the world?"

"I *don't* understand you."

"That makes two of us. How did you ever get to be a supervisor around here without knowing anything?" He stood back, the better to stare up at her. The woman was several inches taller than he was, a disconcerting height. "You pink women *are* running this crazy place, aren't you? Well, then, you should know the score." Owen examined the tiny brown spot on the tip of her nose that could be a freckle. "Where did *I* come from, anyway, and how did I get here? Where is here? How did I get mixed up in this zombie business?"

"There is something terribly wrong here."

"You can say that again."

"But why should I repeat it?"

"Oh, go fly a kite!" He put up a quick hand to stop her question. "I know, I *know*—what is a kite? Don't ask." Owen shook his head in bewilderment. "This is one crazy place! *No* organization all the way down the line. Honey, if the President heard about this town, he'd blow a gasket and send in the marines." Owen gave a despairing wave of hand. "Around *this* town, the war effort is going to hell in a bucket. Hitler must be laughing in his sleep."

She said, "I need to know more about you."

"Let's both start over again." And he reached for her breast identification.

She stepped away from his hand. "Stop that. You are not supposed to touch me. Do you remember your name?"

"Owen Hall."

"And you are twenty-eight?"

"Sure am."

"When did you cease being twenty-eight?"

He said, "When the—" and came up short, astonished at her question and at his attempt to answer. "When—"

She prodded. "When what?"

"I don't know," he confessed after a long minute of introspection. "I just don't know. I *thought* I knew, but when I tried to say it, I lost it. I really don't know."

"Think about it." She watched him carefully.

Owen poked about in the black cavern that used to be his memory. He pried and teased the blackness, searching for any familiar thing. After a long while something moved in the cavern, some vague object having almost familiar lines, and he tried to focus on it. Concentration: it was an automobile! More than that, it was a specific automobile, and he thought he knew it. Owen studied the harder and watched the vehicle take shape with an agonizing slowness.

"A truck! It's a nineteen forty Ford panel job. I see it!"

"What is that object?"

"I drove a nineteen forty Ford panel job—that's a truck with paneled sides. You ride in it, haul things in it."

"Did you haul things in it?"

"Well, of course I—"

He peered hard at the new memory, trying to see and recognize the load in the truck. There was nothing to reward him, nothing beyond those vague but recognizable

lines of a Ford panel job. Owen couldn't even peer inside
the cab; he was unable to ascertain who was driving the
truck. It was a most frustrating memory.

"I can't see anything more," he said ruefully.

"Are you connected with the truck?"

"I think I owned it. I guess I drove it."

"Do you remember anything before the door? Before
you came through the green door this morning?"

"Nope, nothing at all. That old bat just shoved me
through it. Lordy, she was drunk!"

"And you don't know the location of that door?"

"I haven't the foggiest idea."

"Where will you spend the night?"

That gave him pause. "Well, I don't know. I hadn't
even thought about that." Owen scanned the roadside,
looking first along the row houses and then away to the
empty prairie. "You got any park benches around here?"

"What is a park bench?"

A dismal nod. "That's what I thought—I could see it
coming. Honeybee, *whatever* happened to Indiana? The
one I used to live in?"

"Is Indiana a town? I don't know that name."

"Ah, skip it. You don't know any more than I don't
know. Me and Sam Bass, we come from Indiana."

The woman said briskly, "You are instructed to come
to my house tonight. You cannot be permitted to roam
around and you must have a place to sleep. Do you fully
understand me? It is important that you understand me."

Owen's jaw dropped. "Do you really mean that?"

"Certainly. You have to sleep somewhere indoors. You
will stay overnight with me while I attempt to correct your
flaws. You have been improperly reconstructed."

Owen stole a glance at the men riding nearby. "Won't
people talk?"

"Talk about what?"

"Honey, this sure as hell *ain't* Indiana!"

"Do you clearly understand what I am saying? There
must be no more confusion. I insist upon orderliness."

"I read you, baby doll, I *read* you. Your house tonight
—I'll be there with bells on."

"Bells aren't necessary."

The tall blonde gave Owen a metallic plate about the
size of a business card. He moved his thumb across it, in-
wardly pleased with his newfound reading skill. The plate

repeated the legend he'd already read on her steel bar, and immediately below that line was another, bearing a house number—at least, he guessed it was the number to one of the doors along the rolling road.

The wonderment was still in his voice. "Gotcha! And you want *me* to spend the night with *you*."

"Precisely that. It has become necessary. I want to examine you in detail. There is more than a suspicion that you are incomplete. Your present behavior isn't normal and needs correcting." Again she bent down to study the pupils of his eyes. "Do you understand me? Do you read my number? Are my instructions clear?"

Owen returned the study with a keen interest. Her face and her freckle were so close he wanted to stand up on his toes and kiss one or the other, but caution stopped him. A rash act now might spoil the night to come.

"Honeybee, I've memorized your number. I *know* what to do, believe me—I'm no tenderfoot. I'll watch out for a jug, and maybe I can teach you to dance."

"Obey your previous instructions," the woman said. "Report to my house when you are dismissed from work."

The tall pink warden left him without a further word, swinging off the road to take up a stance on somebody's walk before a door. She crossed her arms and began studying the zombies as they rolled by, watching over them like a guardian or a traffic policeman eyeing drivers.

Owen turned around and watched her out of sight. Her pink-clad figure was magnificent. After a while he pulled himself from an anticipatory dream and found himself staring into the face of a workman riding the road.

The man stared blankly at him, seemingly unaware of his existence.

"You poor sap," Owen said. "The trouble with you is, you're all there. Know what I mean?"

The workman hung his head to stare at his feet.

Three

The dullards were leaving the road. They dropped off in twos and threes, in groups of a dozen or more, and at one point nearly a hundred of them quit the roadway together. They knew their destinations.

The endless row of houses with painted doors had given way to an endless row of industrial buildings with open doors—to factories, or warehouses, or chewing gum sweatshops for all Owen knew. There were no neon signs or billboards to advertise their wares, there was nothing to suggest a product, and the drab buildings may have housed arsenals, foundries, power stations, or tin mines. Some one of those featureless buildings may have turned out the rolling road, while the building next door may have manufactured the invisible wheels or the air jets to keep the road moving. Owen's nose failed to detect the scent of a brewery or a distillery.

Every man, every group stepped off the rolling road and vanished through some doorway, not to emerge again. They plodded to work as lifelessly as walking matchsticks. Owen Hall thought it wise to practice safety in numbers: he followed the hundred men through an oversized doorway, while yet others left the road and followed him.

A factory, Owen decided. An outsized factory.

In that first curious look around the place he saw what appeared to be hundreds of machines of totally alien design, machines geared to produce some product that was equally alien. His long years of reading *Amazing Mechanics* magazines failed to provide him with a clue. There were no scraps of anything on the floors to hint at the product and no stockpiles of raw materials at hand waiting to be fashioned into something. He found no sawdust or oil drippings. There was nothing—nothing but the bulky machines aligned row upon row along wide aisles, reaching from one end of the building to the other. The machines hulked over the workmen in monolithic masses with the topsides reaching almost to the roof of the factory.

Owen didn't think the factory manufactured snoods or hairnets for the pink ladies.

The incoming workmen pushed past him, ignoring him, and scattered throughout the building to take up positions before the machines. Each man chose his own machine with a ready familiarity and stood before it, staring at it, awaiting some instruction or signal. There was no talking between them and they appeared to wait without interest or motion, prepared to stand and stare forever if need be.

"I give up on you guys—I just give up." Owen addressed the nearest worker, a balding fellow who would not answer back. "Not one of you—not *one* of you has got sense enough to pour beer out of a boot. What kind of a union you got here, anyway?"

The workmen silently studied their machines.

Owen walked a hundred feet along the nearest aisle until he judged he was at about the center of the building.

"Hey! Is anybody home?" His shout echoed about the cavernous walls.

The soulless workmen didn't turn to stare at the distractor or cover their ears to close out his shouting. They did nothing but stolidly stand and wait.

"Where's the boss? Where's the union steward?"

The zombies studied the massive machinery.

Owen cupped his hands to make a megaphone.

"Fire!"

The zombies were unimpressed.

Another shout: "All right, everybody out! We're going out on strike. Everybody to the picket lines!"

The workmen declined to strike.

Owen uttered a discouraging word.

A whistle shrilled somewhere in the depths of the cavernous factory, and the zombies obediently moved. They bellied up to their machines and leaned against them, resting their foreheads against them, and seemed to go to sleep. That was all. Owen was thunderstruck. No wheels turned, no gears clanked or whirred, no motors raced or strained under a load. Each man appeared to be asleep standing up, using his machine as a kind of pillow. Owen had to admit that was a pretty good job to latch onto—of course, a stool *would* be handy when a man got tired.

He turned around, seeking the whistler. A sudden flash of pink—baby pink—was glimpsed in the distance, and he knew what was coming. His third encounter of the morning and the day was still young. The woman came along the aisle on the run, panting with the unaccustomed exertion. A whistle dangled from a cord about her neck.

"Who did that?" she demanded.

"Who did what?"

"Who shouted?"

"Me, Owen Hall. I'll shout at anybody." He didn't bother to explain the President's Four Freedoms.

"What is the matter here? Why did you raise your voice? Why aren't you working?"

"Which answer do you want first?"

"Be quiet!"

"Well, now, Granny, make up your mind."

Owen inspected the newcomer, but he wasn't impressed. *This* specimen of the pink squad was a distinct disappointment, and he didn't try to conceal that judgment; this one was a far cry from the attractive traffic warden, and again removed from the drunken woman of the doorway. *This* was a much older woman than any he'd seen thus far. She was gray haired, gray eyed, gray skinned, and—he suspected—gray tempered. She was singularly straight up and down inside her coveralls and utterly without humor; she could qualify as somebody's unkindly old grandmother. The woman was shortened or wizened with age, standing no taller than he did. Owen counted that a plus.

"We don't raise our voices in here, man." Her enunciation of *man* contained a built-in gibe.

"Grandmaw, except for you and me nobody in here *has* a voice."

That brought a hostile frown to the gray forehead. She raised her hand to slap him, but changed her mind in mid-thought and instead jabbed at the identification bar pinned under his pocket flap. The bar was roughly pushed into his chest, but this time Owen had no desire to reciprocate.

"I might have known it. A new one." The gray lips curled in scorn. "Didn't they teach you manners?"

"What are manners?" he asked in secret delight.

Grandmother managed a double take and Owen thought it as good, as meaningful as anything Franklin Pangborn had done on the screen.

"Who was your fabricator?"

"My what?"

"Who was responsible for you this morning?"

"Oh, you mean that crazy babe who kicked me out of the house. Well, now, she didn't introduce herself. She was hitting the bottle, see, one of the kind who booze it up and then want to fight. Lousy drinker. Stingy, too—she kept it all to herself." Owen clucked his disapprobation. "But don't worry, Granny, I've got another date tonight."

"You have a what?"

"A place to sleep, a bed warmer." Owen fished out of his pocket and handed over the metallic business card the traffic warden had given him. "This dolly told me to come to her place tonight. I think she's going to give me the works."

"I should hope so," the gray lady retorted. She read the card with her thumb and gave it back to Owen. "It is obvious that you are flawed."

"That's what people keep telling me. They want me to be like the rest of these stiffs."

"Close your mouth and come with me."

Owen closed his mouth and followed the gray woman along the aisle to an unattended machine. In the next five minutes he was introduced to the production line and it was confounding.

The machine itself was a monstrous, hulking thing the size of a highway truck—two trucks, when one considered the height, with one truck stacked atop the other and the whole nearly reaching to the factory roof. Almost all the working parts were concealed from view behind the casing, hiding any wheels and gears from curious eyes and at the same time preventing him or those mindless workmen from sticking their fingers into the works. The front face of the machine occupied the same position as the tailgate of the highway truck, and that face had the only visible working parts. There was a small window embedded in the face and a short row of push buttons below the window. A stainless steel bar was positioned above the window. The bar was about five inches wide and two inches high, of concave design, and set into the machine casing at the height of a man's head.

Owen discovered that it was intended to receive a man's head—his forehead.

Following the gray lady's explicit instructions, he bellied up to the machine just as the other men had done, placed his forehead against the curved bar, and poised an index finger above the row of buttons.

"Now what?"

"Visualize a slice of bacon."

"Do *what?*" He turned around to stare.

She pushed his head against the machine. "Think bacon!"

Owen thought about a slice of bacon. When he had formed a complete picture in his mind, when he had visualized the image of a single slice of bacon fairly oozing with vitamins and protein and goodness, he pushed the first numbered button and the machine went into operation. A light blinked on inside the window and a little paper tray slid out of a side opening to position itself in the center of the working area. A single strip of bacon dropped down from somewhere overhead—from a height about equal to the steel bar where his forehead rested—and fell onto the tray. The machine waited.

Owen stepped back to stare at his handiwork. "Well, call me Chester White!"

"Don't stop," the woman snapped. "Continue the job. You haven't completed the ration."

"Say, that's a damned good trick. How'd I do it?"

"It is reconstituted pork. You visualized it by memory and the production unit solidified the visualization."

"Is it real bacon? Edible?"

"Of course it is. Now follow my instructions. Keep on working."

Again he bellied up to the machine and fitted his forehead into the concave bar to think bacon. Another slice as succulent as the first dropped from overhead. Owen kept at it until he had five tasty slices resting in the paper tray—a triumph of mind over matter. The bacon looked so good he was immediately hungry.

The woman said, "That is enough. Now wrap it."

Pressing the number two button with a feeling of secret exhilaration, Owen watched through the window as a sheet of waxed paper spewed from the side opening, wrapped itself around the tray of bacon with an assist from a pair of mechanical fingers reaching down from above, and tidied up the package for someone's breakfast in the morning.

"Dispatch it."

He pushed the third button and the package was whisked out of sight. An empty tray slid into position and waited for the young creator's next visualization.

"Neat, very neat. I didn't even say *shazam*."

"Stop that noise. Talking isn't permitted here. Continue working until the shift has ended."

"You mean this is all I have to do?"

"Isn't it enough?"

"Well, yeah, I guess so."

"Then do it, and keep your mouth shut."

The gray woman watched over his shoulder for the next several minutes, making certain he did a competent job. The product must have been satisfactory, since she said nothing more. He felt like a merchant prince.

Owen thought bacon, made bacon, wrapped bacon, and sent bacon on its way to some unknown place, five slices to the package. All of his bacon was of the finest quality, prime meat, because it had occurred to him that one of those packages might be his breakfast in the morning and he would surely be hungry if the charming pink-and-blonde creature lived up to her promise. Bacon fit for kings and queens fell from overhead—sprang from his forehead, in a manner of speaking—and filled the trays to be carried away. Owen admired the way the waxed paper appeared from nowhere and wrapped itself about the meat; he admired the dexterity of the slim mechanical fingers that reached down from above to finish the packaging. Owen recognized those fingers as a form of waldoes. They'd been invented by the same man who invented the rolling road, and both inventions were duly reported in the science-wonder magazines.

After a while the gray woman left him, mumbling her grudging satisfaction with his work. She failed to say thank you.

Owen watched her out of sight, watched from the corner of his eye until he was certain she was gone and not merely hiding somewhere to mousetrap him. When the woman didn't immediately come back to spy on him, Owen quit work and walked over to see what the next fellow was making.

Bacon. It was poor bacon compared to his own, and Owen guessed the man didn't have his mind on the job—or didn't have enough of a mind for the job. He continued the inspection of the nearby machines and their products. Several workmen were making bacon, but the quality of the meats varied widely from one man to another. A few were turning out slices of ham, thin stringy ham that looked less appetizing than the poor-grade bacon. One man was dispatching empty trays. Each tray was neatly wrapped in waxed paper and sent on its way, but it contained nothing. Owen figured the guy for a politician.

Two men who worked at machines next to each other were making slices of white bread, and to Owen's gaze it seemed very good bread indeed—not the barely edible sliced cardboard found in some restaurants. Perhaps the workmen were professional bakers. Near them a man made butter or margarine, but it was impossible to determine which. Owen decided not to have butter on his toast in the morning.

He found the egg factory just before returning to his own machine. A small egg tray with room for just two eggs rested on the bottom of the work area, and the mechanical fingers reached down from above with an egg carefully cradled in each hand—if they could be called hands. The eggs weren't allowed to drop, but were placed in the cartons, closed, tied with string, and sent on their way. The egg man had his heart in his work.

Owen returned to his station.

He turned out bacon like the skilled professional that he suddenly was, uncounted slices of succulent bacon hav-

ing less fat than any other production unit along the aisle.
Somebody would thank him in the morning for the tasty
breakfasts *he* was preparing, while somebody else next
door would surely express their envy at the superior product when compared to the grungy stuff *they* were eating.
Perhaps that second party would even launch an investigation and then demand new standards of workmanship
so that all bacon would be as good as his. *His* was clearly
the superior product and would be the envy of many
households.

Then Owen made a necktie.

It wasn't a very good necktie. The colors were poor
and the pattern was awry, but it was his—the very first
necktie he'd ever made—and he was quietly proud of it.
He wondered if perhaps he could create a fad for neckties among the populace, something to relieve the monot-
ony of the drab coveralls. He made several neckties, each
an improvement over the one before with better and truer
colors, distinctive patterns, and eye-catching designs—all
in the correct width of course. Each necktie was wrapped
in individual gift packages and sent on its way.

Next he tried a loaf of bread and discovered what the
fourth and last button on the row was for. The bread was
a dismal failure and had to be scrubbed; his visualization
of the interior was faulty and the loaf sagged like a wet
shirt wadded into a ball. Clearly, it wasn't fit to eat. Curious as to how to be rid of the mistake, Owen punched the
last button in the row—a red button—and the faulty
bread dropped from sight. He thought he saw a little door
open at the far end of the chamber, and the bread seemed
to fall through it. Well and good. The working area behind the window—and suddenly he thought of it as his
operating theater—was given a steam bath from pipes or
vents not in his line of sight, and then other pipes un-
leashed a furious gale of air that dried the operating theater. When the scrubbing was complete and his theater
once again sterile, the work light went out and the machine stopped.

Owen pushed the first button and made ready to begin
all over again. The light came on and a tray slid into position, awaiting his inspired creation. Owen put his forehead firmly against the concave bar and thought about a
cigar—the kind of cigar he liked, the kind he used to
smoke back there.

A worm turned in his mind and asked, Back *where?*

"Well, you know," he answered aloud. "Back there where I used to be, before this happened."

Before *what* happened, the nag worm demanded?

"Before I stopped being twenty-eight," Owen said. "I used to be alive and twenty-eight. There was a war on and I was draft bait, and all that there stuff."

Were you in the war? the nagging memory asked.

Owen paused in his work to consider that. "No, I wasn't," he said at last. "And I'm alive now. I'm trying to make a cigar."

He closed his eyes to concentrate on the cigar. It must be firm, but long and slim, having a greenish brown wrapper and a decent filler free of weeds. Not a fat cigar and not a blunt one—he found those kind too strong. And it should cost more than a nickel. He may as well go the whole hog while he was dreaming.

Owen opened his eyes to examine the tray. "Wow!"

He was so pleased with the cigar that he made a dozen more in rapid succession, and then concentrated on a dozen matches to light the cigars—but, on second thought, whipped up two dozen matches because his cigars frequently went out. He was in business for himself.

His work came to a full and unhappy stop when Owen realized what would happen if he pressed the second button or the third: his fine cigars would scuttle away to become somebody's breakfast. He stepped away from the machine to take stock, and then peered about to ascertain if he was being watched by the gray granny. The woman wasn't in sight. Owen began hunting for a door, for a way into the sealed operating theater of his magic manufacturing machine. It seemed logical to him that some kind of entrance should be available; the matches and cigars *had* to be retrieved.

He began the search at the corner on his left hand, working all along the side of the great machine to its far end. The end of it was just across an aisle from another machine and another worker, and that end surface was totally blank—there wasn't so much as a seam or a rivet. Owen went back to the front window and started again on the opposite flank, fingering the vast expanse of metal from the right-hand corner rearward. He found a small door secured by a latch. Owen turned the latch and pulled the door open, seeing the work light blink out as he did so: a safety switch was connected to the door. He made haste to recover his prized cigars and the matches, tucking them away in his breast pockets. Owen closed the clean-out door and retreated to his rightful position at the front window, a satisfied smile on his face. He was a self-supporting small businessman.

Next, a bottle of good booze. It had to be *good* booze —not like that raw stuff the first woman had been belting down. Well, why not two bottles while he was at it? He thought that pint bottles would fit into his pants pockets very well indeed; they were large pockets.

Owen bellied up to the machine, put his forehead to the operating bar, and very carefully visualized his twin desires. Two fine pint bottles of clear glass. Very good. Now to the contents. He struggled to recreate the liquid contents just as he'd last seen them—it—on the shelf of Ollie Cronin's drugstore in Hartford City, Indiana. The contents must be a golden brown—but a shade more golden than brown; they—or it—must be smooth to the taste, yet fiery and full bodied; the liquid should be a sour mash whiskey of, say, ninety proof and eight years old. Yes, eight was a nice round number. He put his fine mind to it and sweated the recreation. His imagination said, Let it be choice.

Owen pushed the first button and opened his eyes.

Two perfect pints of whiskey waited on the tray in his operating theater. One of the bottles had fallen over, but as he watched the mechanical fingers came down and righted it. The lids were on tight. Owen felt pleased. He suspected that he had a surprise for the baby doll who awaited him at home that night. Owen stashed the bottles in his pockets and got back to the front of the machine a moment before the gray grandmother hove into sight.

He dutifully resumed turning out juicy bacon.

The woman paused at his shoulder for a sullen moment and inspected his product—neat packages of rich, tasty bacon. Five slices to the package, all nicely wrapped and sealed and sent on their way to the breakfast tables.

He stayed at the task as long as the woman stood behind him, but when she was again satisfied and went on her way Owen made a monkey wrench.

It had occurred to him that a fine monkey wrench might please someone so he visualized one, produced it, wrapped it, and sent it along after the bacon. The wrench had been a good one, a fine tool surely to be appreciated by a conscientious craftsman, and he was pleased with his handiwork. Good tools made good mechanics.

Other tools followed, sometimes one to a package and sometimes several just for variety: screwdrivers, pliers, ball peen hammers, chisels, a crosscut saw and then a fine-toothed one, awls, squares, files, center punches, steel rules—but he *did* worry about getting the inch marks the proper distance apart—an an adze. A hatchet was an afterthought. He made everything a journeyman carpenter or a mechanic might want in his toolbox. He made toolboxes. The quality and workmanship of his tools evoked a mild wonder: they were so well made, so finely balanced, so meticulous in detail, so *right*. Perhaps *he'd* been a carpenter or a mechanic before.

Before what?

Before he ceased being twenty-eight, before the fuzzy image of the Ford panel truck, before he died.

Owen stopped work to think about that.

Scrawny wisps of memory scuttled about in his mind, skittering away in maddening fashion when he tried to pin them down. Sometimes two or three stray wisps touched and thereafter clung together, stayed together to form a whole, but in the next moment two similar wisps rebounded from each other and refused to be joined. Here and there he discovered half an image, half a memory. There were vague and mysterious things in the back of his mind, mysterious shapes that seemed related to the darting strays, but they too refused to assume a solid shape and hold for his inspection. It was a frustrating business, but his mind didn't seem to be all there; his memory seemed to be like the scrawny bacon made by the joes down the line.

He easily remembered Cronin's drugstore and the booze on the shelves. He remembered Hartford City and now he supposed that he'd once lived there. And he recalled the truck—the 1940 Ford panel truck was clearly fixed.

Owen studied that image.

The truck wasn't new: he hadn't owned or driven a new truck. It appeared to be two, or three, or maybe four years old, now that he examined it. Suppose that it was three years old and *he* had driven it. That meant he was alive and driving in 1943. So far, so good. That fitted with other stray facts he remembered. Franklin Roosevelt was President of the United States—oh, yes, yes, he was serving his third term as President, and there was a war on. *That* was right. The United States was fighting a war with Germany and Italy and . . . and who? Some other country. The armies were fighting on two fronts—but where?

Everybody was pitching into the war effort. Many of the factories employed two shifts and some even had three—they were running twenty-four hours around the clock, making planes and jeeps and shells and nuts and bolts, and piling up the overtime. Did he get any overtime?

Owen didn't know. He couldn't force his half-memory to tell him.

He felt so frustrated he put his forehead to the machine and made a cucumber. He was fond of cucumbers.

Owen Hill was surprised at the shortness of the workday. It had union hours beat handily.

He guessed that it was still several hours before noon when the grayhaired supervisor took up a stance in the middle of the factory and blew another piercing blast on her whistle. The blast stopped the works. The zombies stood away from their machines. Owen pushed the red button to clear the operating theater of a cabbage head he was working on and wandered into the aisle. The shrill whistle echoed around the building a second time, but Owen was the only man to cover his ears. He discovered the wooden workers trooping out the door and followed them for want of anything better to do. There was no point in hanging about the factory and getting into another argument with Granny.

The rolling road was still moving in its original direction, although he'd half expected to find it reversed. That meant he—and all the others—would have to ride all the way around the town on the great circle tour until they reached their respective doors again. Mighty poor planning, he thought. This was an inefficient way to run things with a war on. He tried to remember if that inventor fellow—what was his name?—had arranged for a reversal of the road when it was time to go home.

Owen mounted the road with considerably more skill than he'd managed the first and second times and felt proud of himself. He was becoming expert. There was a moment of awkwardness when he thought the road would throw him, but he held his balance and remained upright. The zombies rode home as emotionless as before, displaying neither surprise nor exhilaration at the brevity of their workday. Perhaps this was the usual day—perhaps they were used to short hours and no overtime.

Own looked back at the factory a last time.

The elderly gray woman stood in the enormous doorway and the hostile gray eyes followed his departure with some suspicion. She was obviously upset about something, and her manner suggested that *he* was the cause of the trouble; her suspicious glare followed him nearly out of sight. He couldn't guess at the cause of her upset; certainly nothing had gone wrong at the factory to his knowledge.

Owen suppressed a sudden notion to turn around and wiggle his fingers at her—she just might have sharp eyesight and note where he was holding his thumb. She just might understand the parting gesture.

He decided not to go home, not to beat a retreat to the nice blonde's house just then. That could wait a while. There would be plenty of time for the pink lady's company at nightfall. The sun was stiflingly hot and approaching the zenith, but he knew of a cool place to escape from that sun, an inviting place where he could sample his homemade wares and contemplate the mysteries of the universe—or, at least, the mysteries that were rocking about in his skull. The blonde would keep, but the timber beckoned him.

Four

Caskets!—a vile modern phrase, which compels a person
of sense and good taste to shrink more disgustfully than ever
before from the idea of being buried at all.

—Nathaniel Hawthorne

The woodlands were everything that Owen Hall had
anticipated and he plunged into the cooling shade with
ready delight. The trees smelled good; they smelled of
Indiana during his boyhood.

Owen had kept a careful watch on his tedious circle of
the town, half expecting to see the drunken harridan
again as he traveled past her door—whichever green door
that might be—and fully expecting to meet up with the
blonde date a second time, but neither woman was
sighted. He deemed it wise to avoid both women on the
circle tour, since both were likely to cause him trouble.

There had been other traffic wardens dressed in pink
coveralls watching the workmen ride past their stations,
but all were strangers to him. Owen thought he detected
surprise on some of their faces, but he kept his head
down and his mouth shut and did nothing to call attention to himself. He didn't want to be shunted away from
his goal, so he rode as the zombies did, with his gaze
firmly fastened on the nape of the neck in front of him.
When in Indianapolis, do as the Indians do.

He tried to ignore the scorching heat of the sun and

concentrate on what was ahead of him. The cemetery—
that first familiar landmark—finally came into sight and
he made ready to leave the road. Men were still at work
in the old graveyard, but Owen ignored them and kept a
sharp lookout for anything clad in pink. A careful side-
long scrutiny revealed that his immediate area was free
of the wardens.

Owen jumped from the road. He stumbled in the tall
grass, grabbed a breast pocket to prevent the cigars from
falling out, recovered his balance, and broke into a trot.
There was no outcry behind him, no frantic blowing of
whistles.

The leafy timber seemed to welcome him.

Owen paused just inside the tree line and turned to look
back along his trail, but he wasn't being followed, and the
zombies appeared not to miss him. It was comforting to
know that they weren't likely to snitch on him. Owen
worked his way deeper into the woods, always looking
for, but failing to find, sign of bird or animal life. The
timber floor was moss covered and thick with weeds and
underbrush, but he saw no evidence of game trails or
man-made ploddings. Perhaps this part of the new world
was unexplored by woman or workman. Well, that was
their loss.

Owen found a place to his liking alongside an aged
locust. It was a familiar tree. He cleared away the brush
and stomped the weeds flat to make a sitting place and
then relaxed with his back against the locust. Little of the
outside world was visible except ragged splotches of sun
and sky overhead. It was pleasant to be alone for a bit.

The two pint bottles were lumps in his pockets.

Owen laid one bottle aside—for the blonde, he told
himself—and held the other up against a shaft of filtered
sunlight. A nod of satisfaction. The contents of the bottle
certainly looked smooth, and he was pleased to note his
visualizing had been so successful that a tax stamp sealed
the cap. Now *that* was artistic recreation. Owen broke the
seal and removed the cap.

He opened his eyes a swallow later and was amazed
at what he had wrought. A second swallow quickly followed, accompanied by a growing admiration of the
product.

"By golly, that *is* smooth!"

The whiskey warmed his stomach. He glanced toward

the sky and accidentally discovered a companion—a gray squirrel perched on an overhanging limb of a nearby tree, peering down at him with open curiosity. Owen was elated by the discovery: there *was* another live body in the woods beside his own.

"Hi, there, old squirrel. Want a nip?"

The animal studied him in silence. It showed no sign of fear and Owen thought that a good omen.

"It's good booze," he assured the rodent, and sighted through the bottle to admire the golden color. "Made it myself in one of those fancy think-and-do machines. That old bat who kicked me out of the house this morning could take lessons from *me*." Owen tilted the bottle to his lips a third time, pleased with what the liquid was doing inside.

To the squirrel: "Are you reconstituted pork, or are you the real thing?"

The animal switched its tail and watched him, and Owen decided it was the real thing. He'd never heard of a zombie squirrel.

He placed the bottle between his knees to prevent spillage and went to his breast pocket for matches and a cigar. The result was less than satisfactory, a sorry reversal of his whiskey-making skills; one or two pulls on the cigar told him the quality of his craftsmanship wasn't all that good. But make do, make do—there was a war on, and the cigars could have been so rank as to be unsmokable. As poor as they were, they weren't as bad as Ramses, and most places, Ramses was all a man could find when he wanted a smoke.

"Easily worth a nickel, I'd say—but, then, I don't think I'd pay a dime for it. It's not worth a dime."

Owen decided to smoke it through to the end and search for ways to improve the product. Perhaps later samples would be better—perhaps this one cigar was the first of the batch and his early visualization had been faulty.

He rested easily against the locust tree with the bottle in one hand and the cigar in the other to take stock of a distant life—his first life, the life before this one, when he had been twenty-eight years old and had driven, or at least owned, a 1940 Ford truck. Phantom ideas prowled around inside his skull, mere shadows of ancient memories. He prodded those vague stirrings, teased and poked at the wispy ghosts to force them into shapes he could examine and just perhaps recognize. The shadows were there for his inspection if only he could make them stand and be counted. Odd ideas and old ideas of shapes and things had been recurring all morning while he traveled and worked, and he wanted to see old faces, old scenes, old tools that he knew. That cucumber had turned out nicely in the machine, which proved that the memories *were* there—somewhere.

There was a war on.

Franklin Roosevelt was the President of the United States. He was serving his third term in the White House, and some Republicans had taken to calling him King Franklin. Henry Wallace was the Vice-President, and those same Republicans were calling *him* some pretty nasty names. The Republicans had lost a lot of elections.

Because of the war the country was making do with less of everything; butter and sugar and meat and tires and gasoline were rationed—although a person could always find what he wanted on the black market if, say, he was willing to pay fifty cents a gallon for bootleg gasoline. Owen had good tires on his panel truck; there was no immediate worry about rubber, and when he remembered to keep his speed down, the truck consistently delivered more than twenty miles to the gallon, except in Indianapolis. That town was hard on man, beast, and automobile.

Owen nipped at the bottle and considered the facts— those few new memories he accepted as facts.

St. Louis had won the World Series last October, handily beating New York four games to one. Now *those* were red-letter days! The final game was played in New York on October fifth; therefore it should be *winter* now, not this blazing summer day in July or August. Because St. Louis won *last* October—a few months ago—it should be January or February or maybe March, 1943, right now. Today. This timber and the surrounding prairie should be blanketed by snow with an underlayer of ice. He *did* remember that. The winter was firmly fixed in mind because it followed the St. Louis victory—the first time the St. Louis team had even been in the Series since 1934. During one night of that winter a sleet storm came first,

beginning shortly after midnight, and snow started falling
a few hours later.

Owen paused to review those new memories, and was
satisfied they weren't false ones. Roosevelt *was* serving
his third term, and Wallace *was* next in line. Wallace had
been an Iowa farm boy before he fell in with politicians,
but he hadn't always been the Vice-President. Somebody
named Garner came first—ah, John Garner. Old John
was Vice-President during Roosevelt's first and second
terms, but people grumbled about his age and his evil
habits, so Roosevelt had sent him home to Texas and
picked Wallace in the . . . the 1940 election. That felt
right and sounded right: the 1940 election. And meanwhile there was a war going on in Europe. Hitler was
thrashing everybody.

The United States fell into the war the very next year,
1941. Japan. Now *there* was the other name that had
eluded him. The Japanese fleet and air force attacked
Pearl Harbor on a Sunday in December and suddenly the
United States was into all the wars: in Europe, in Africa,
and in the Pacific Ocean. That's what happened.

He was twenty-eight; he'd been born in 1915.

That automatically made him draft bait, and only a
couple of years ago he'd gone down to the schoolhouse in
Hartford City along with sixteen million other guys and
registered for the draft. Congress had passed a law con-
scripting just about every male who wasn't lame or blind
or hiding out in the hills, and on some nameless October
day in 1940 he'd lined up before a teacher's desk to regis-
ter. One of his former grammar school teachers had
signed him on and pretended to recognize him when he
recited his name and address and gave her a friendly
hello. The schoolhouse had been packed with bait like
himself, and for all he knew, the teacher recognized all
of them. She had been there a mighty long time, teaching
the same grade.

Well, now, where did all that leave him?

It left him with a cold cigar and a warm bottle. Owen
sampled the bottle's contents, congratulated himself again
on his skill, and relit the cigar.

He rather suspected that he'd been a carpenter back
there in that fuzzy life behind him. The tools he'd made
from instinct or memory had all seemed of a professional
quality—unlike the cigar—and they were the kind of

tools he'd want to own and use himself. And he owned the kind of panel truck a carpenter might drive. It seemed to him now that the truck was painted a dark green, or maybe black.

Concentrate on that truck: it's the key.

It wasn't a new truck, of course, because it had been built in 1940—or perhaps late 1939—and he was driving it during his twenty-eighth year in January or February or maybe March, 1943. Had he bought it new? No answer, no memory. Well, then, a used truck—a convenient panel job for an honest carpenter going about his business. Abruptly, Owen saw himself sitting in the truck and peered closer. A shadowy image crawled from a hole in the depths of his mind and raised itself for inspection. He was driving the truck and there was something on the seat beside him. A passenger? No answer, no memory. Owen poked at the stray memory to see it move and re-form to his advantage. The scene became clear.

He was driving the truck, and it was snowing.

He was certain it was snowing because now he could see the snowfall in his headlights, and the headlights were lit because it was still dark outside—not yet sunrise. The image was extraordinarily clear. The sleet storm had come first, beginning around midnight or a little later, and the snow fell on top of it a few hours later. Owen prodded the memory. He studied it from the viewpoint of an interested bystander and realized that he was driving to work on an ice- and snow-covered road somewhere near Hartford City. He was driving cautiously, knowing what was under his wheels and knowing the treachery of ice.

Another vagrant ghost of an idea squirmed in his mind, and the 1943 Owen turned his head to look down at the box of carpenter's tools on the seat beside him, a large and heavy box filled with two or three hundred dollars' worth of tools—just about his only asset other than the truck. In his mind's eye—no, his mind's ear—he heard again the bleating locomotive horn and the muffled rumbling of a freight train on the Pennsy tracks. The train was shockingly close.

Owen Hall sat up straight and took a very long pull on the bourbon. He knew with sudden certainty how, and why, and when he ceased being twenty-eight on a wretched February date in 1943.

The red flashers were working: he could see them

blinking in rapid one-two fashion through the snowstorm. His brakes were working and he knew how to use them on snow or ice, but this time the gentle pumping motions didn't bring the truck to a controlled stop in a straight line. The rear wheels swung from under him, swung the truck sideways despite his efforts to steer in control, while he and it continued traveling forward in the original direction. The icy road thwarted him. Owen caught a frantic glimpse of the red flashing lights coming at him against a side window, then going over his head, over the truck roof—and then the truck slammed broadside against the Pennsy freight. His time sense slowed to near zero.

He didn't hear a sound of impact and thought that strange. There should have been a thumping smack at the broad point of collision, but he heard only a scraping noise that couldn't be readily identified. The truck was being carried along with the train, carried pell mell along the right-of-way. The red flashers were down and they, together with the pole, were being dragged along with him. Owen watched the drainage ditch flash by alongside his window and then saw the newly splintered side of a boxcar through the opposite window, on the passenger side. His truck and the boxcar seemed to be joined; they hurtled forward together along the Pennsy tracks. The strange scraping noise sped along with them. He knew that the truck headlights were still on. He held to the wheel.

Owen turned his head again to look down at the box of carpenter's tools on the seat beside him. The lid was open and the tools were flying about inside his cab. A crosscut saw lay in his lap, and then he remembered that the saw had bumped against his head and fallen to his lap. A hammer rested on the dashboard, above the speedometer. The toolbox left the seat; it appeared to lift itself and leap forward through the gaping hole where the windshield had been. He hadn't realized the windshield was gone. Snow was coming through the new opening, pelting his face. Owen gripped the wheel tightly, although he had lost steering control, and the snow on his hands was red snow.

The peculiar scraping noise stopped without warning and Owen swung his head to stare at the boxcar. The noise had been coming from the car's wheels, but now the noise was missing, although the boxcar was still there. The car was toppling toward him, pushing the roof in like collapsing cardboard. Owen watched the roof come to him. The boxcar toppled over and fell into the drainage ditch alongside the Pennsy tracks, burying the Ford truck beneath it. There was no sound at all.

That had happened to him.

The squirrel was gone from the overhanging limb.

Owen Hall blinked at the mildness of the . . . the transition, the experience, and wondered why the experience hadn't followed the book. Somebody wasn't playing by the rules, and Pastor Coulson had been dead wrong.

There had been no sharp division of time, no definite and recognizable transition period between *that* night and *this* day: snowstorm gave way to heat of summer in the bat of an eye. Panel truck and boxcar gave way to a green door and a thwack on the rump between breaths. There didn't seem to be as much as a count of one or two between the incident with the freight train and the incident with the boozy broad. There had been no intermission between the acts, and he marveled at that.

Owen had a drink and once again relit the cigar. He'd have to pick up a supply of matches.

This place certainly didn't resemble any kind of heaven or hell that he'd read or heard about, but if it *was* hell, it was a most peculiar hell. No devils, no tails. Pastor Coulson would be most disappointed when he woke up and walked through somebody's door to discover this world. The pastor's promises and predictions had gone awry, and he wouldn't take that lightly.

Owen had seen a dozen or so tall women clad in pink coveralls, who seemed to run the town and all its works, and perhaps two or three hundred male zombies, who worked for the women. He'd seen one live gray squirrel and wanted to imagine there were others in the trees. But there wasn't a pitchfork, a tail, or a pair of angelic wings in the whole lot of them, in all the town.

Well, then, where was he?

The only answer that came to mind was the name of a candy bar: back in the thirties, when he was a kid with no more than a nickel or a dime at a time to spend, there'd been a pretty good candy bar called *Damifino*. That was the only answer to explain the present situation. The town back yonder certainly wasn't Hartford City, In-

diana, in any shape or form; good old H.C. didn't have a
full quota of paved sidewalks, much less a rolling road.
He might still be in Indiana. The prairie and the timber
looked like Indiana, but with all the towns and farms and
service stations taken away. Yes, and the Pennsylvania
tracks were gone, too—all in the space of a few months.
He had stopped being twenty-eight in February and now
a few months later, in July or August, say, all was
changed.

Owen found time to regret the loss of his panel job.
That had been a good truck with good gas mileage and
good rubber—a shame to lose it like that, with little
chance of replacing it until the war was over. The President had stopped almost all passenger car production for
the duration and only enough trucks were being built to
keep the businessmen in business. Detroit was working
overtime turning out jeeps and tanks and cannon for half
the armies of the world, and a man without a car or
truck had to walk or ride the bus—if there were any
buses.

Of course, he didn't need an automobile with the rolling road available to him, but that road only moved
around in a circle, and he didn't really care to travel
around and around the same town for the rest of his life.
The truck could have hauled him across the prairie to the
next town, but lacking a truck he'd just have to walk
when he decided to move on. Move where? Damifino.
He'd keep his overnight date with the blonde babe and go
exploring in the morning. He might find out where he
was, or he might find Hartford City just over the hills a
piece.

Owen stood up and stretched. He felt good, not counting a certain light-headedness.

His whiskey was proving to be of the best quality. He
raised the bottle to his lips to drink, but then paused to
reconsider a phenomenon. *He* drank, but the other men
did not. It was a belated realization, but now it struck him
that none of the zombies in the factory had made a trip
to the drinking fountain all morning. He had not seen a
fountain anywhere in the building. And, for *that* matter,
none of them had gone to the men's room either. It just
wasn't natural.

Owen swallowed the drink and knew that he was natu-

ral. He walked around behind the locust tree to be natural,
although there was no one in sight to watch him. Good
old Indiana boys were just shy.

Owen gouged a shallow hole in the ground with the
heel of his shoe and buried the cigar butt; it would be
dumb to set fire to such a nice place. He pocketed the
second bottle of booze and struck off through the timber,
making for the open prairie away from the town. It was
much too early to go back there, too early to go back to
the nice tall blonde with the freckled nose, and just now
he had a hankering to see big prairie. Maybe that was his
distant past calling him; maybe he was really a Plains
Indian in a paleface body. His grandmother had had high
cheekbones and could sit on her haunches.

Owen plodded along through the weedy underbrush,
satisfied with himself. Those puzzling questions about his
past life had been answered—up to a certain point—and
he knew no more reason to probe there. He'd met up with
a Pennsy freight train on a snowy night, and that answered
that. Perhaps his coming companion of the night could
explain to him why there'd been no intermission between
that life and this one; perhaps she could tell him what
had happened to the months between February and August, and perhaps she could tell him what he was doing
here and just where—or what—here was. He was content
to wait.

The enormity of the prairie took his breath.

A vast and unending sea of grass. Quite literally, it
stretched from one horizon to the other without a visible
break—without a house, barn, silo, or gasoline station.
The prairie was empty of roads, rail trackage, billboards,
or telegraph poles; it revealed neither humans, horses,
cattle, barking dogs, nor the furrows of a plow. There
were no windmills. Thousands of empty acres filled the
world from one far reach of his sight to the other—a
world abounding in the tall grasses that again reminded
him of the buffalo grass his grandfather had talked about.
There were no junkyards.

The whole world seemed empty but for the town behind him, and that enormous vacuity stirred his sense of
wonder. There were no beer signs creaking in the wind.

After a while Owen turned westward and made his
way along the timberline, keeping to the shade for com-

fort. He didn't need to step out onto that prairie to know that it was hotter than the hinges of hell. The heat of the day and the lush growth around him again suggested July or August—a very far cry from that night a few hours ago when he had stopped being twenty-eight. It was a slow walk because of the tangled undergrowth, but not an unpleasant one; he paused two or three—or maybe four—times to eye the great grassland and to sip at his first bottle, continuing to marvel at the quality. Owen was content.

The old cemetery began where the timber ended.

Those ancient gravediggers had started their work at some distant point on the prairie and dug almost to the tree line before stopping. Fallen monuments were visible from where Owen stood in the shade, looking out at the workmen who'd left the road in the early morning. Unlike the factory workers with the shorter hours, these diggers were still at it, industriously spading the cemetery all unmindful of the hot sun. They didn't appear to be sweating. He watched them for a while and fell to wondering why they didn't sweat, didn't stop to wipe a brow or take a breath.

A half-dozen oblong gray boxes were stacked nearby while yet another box rested alongside the hole being dug. Owen thought the boxes more resembled mummy cases with rounded ends than ordinary caskets. They looked plastic.

He took a drink, pocketed the bottle, and ambled over to the open grave.

"Hello, sports. Digging for buried treasure?"

The zombies standing about the excavation ignored him. The pair down in the hole didn't stop work or glance up at the newcomer.

"Do you characters have any idea what you're doing?"

The two men in the hole continued to shovel dirt.

"That's what I thought," Owen said.

He eyed the small group aboveground; they did nothing more than lean on their shovels and watch the pair excavating the grave. Some of them watched the dirt being thrown out of the hole, while others watched the watchers who were watching the dirt. They reminded Owen of the feather merchants in the bad old days of the Depression, when gangs of WPA workers leaned on their shovels for hours, watching one or two new men actually work. It was a novel sight to watch a newcomer work for his pittance. The Republicans had been bitter about that, too.

Owen studied the mummy case caskets. They were much too short to contain the bodies of any woman he'd seen thus far, but they seemed about the right size for the zombies.

He walked around the idle watchers and went along to the newly opened graves they had finished working earlier. Small notches or steps had been cut into the packed clay at one end of each pit, toeholds to enable the excavators to climb in and out, and in addition the men had dropped a gravestone or a broken chunk of marble into each grave as a further assist in climbing. The digs were six feet deep, but seemed narrower than the standard opening.

Owen swung around to again study the stacked boxes that resembled streamlined mummy cases, then looked back into the empty grave at his feet. It wasn't entirely empty. There was debris at the bottom of the hole and something else small and round that gleamed dully in the sun. He'd almost overlooked the tiny object. The unknown something appeared to be a burnt yellow stone or perhaps a sickly orange one—it looked like a fat but dirty pearl.

Owen climbed down into the grave to investigate.

A man's ring. A ring caked with damp clay and covered with mucky debris, but a fine ring nevertheless. He sat down on the marble throne the workmen had left behind and carefully washed the ring with whiskey, then cleaned and dried it on his sleeve. A very nice ring indeed. He thought it might be topaz, or perhaps a yellow sapphire—something quite expensive and much too valuable to be left behind. Someone had been careless.

Owen turned the gem in the sunshine, admiring it. A woman's strident voice sounded somewhere above him.

He got up and crouched on the marble stoop to peer over the edge of the grave. Once again, baby pink; the long arm of the law had arrived. Yet another woman clad in the familiar pink garment stood a short distance away with her back to him, scolding the zombie crew clustered about the working grave. She was agitated and more than a little annoyed. She waved her hands in their faces and let them know her anger; her tone was accusatory.

Owen knew her problem. She had heard him talking, she had overheard him trying to strike up a conversation with the crew while she was lollygagging in the timber, or whatever she was doing in there, and had come out to learn the reason. Talking wasn't permitted among the males.

Owen waited until she ran out of breath. He stood up straight on the marble stoop with his head and shoulders aboveground.

"Hi, there, cupcake! I'm grave-robbing."

The woman spun around in startled disbelief.

Owen looked at her ashen face and then her crumpling body as it tumbled into the weedy grass.

"Now, ain't that just like a woman?" he asked the zombies. "Give them a straight answer and they faint dead away."

Five

Owen Hall couldn't just leave the poor woman lying there in the sun to bake and burn, but she posed a problem.

An unconscious body longer than six feet in length was more than he could manage up and over his shoulder— he couldn't even get the body into a sitting or kneeling position to throw it over his shoulder—so he abandoned the niceties and simply dragged the woman into the shade. Her heels left twin grooves through the fresh dirt.

The stolid workmen watched them go, staring after the pink-clad body as if mesmerized.

"Don't get excited," Owen called, but then realized that not even an earthquake would excite them. "I'm not going to rape her. Why don't you guys come in here and sit down? It's cooler in the shade."

They ignored his kindly invitation.

Owen propped the woman's body against a tree. She fell over. He straightened her up again, but the woman toppled as soon as he took his hands away.

"Well, I never claimed I could win 'em all."

He left the unconscious woman where she lay and went

in search of her resting place, her hideaway. She hadn't been waiting here at the edge of the cemetery when he first stepped out of the timber and strolled over to inspect the graves. They would have seen each other at once— he would have caught the telltale flash of pink as she turned to stare at him. Owen prowled the woods along the borders of the cemetery looking for a trail that might point the way. He suspected that her campgrounds, or office, or whatever she called the lollygagging place would be out of sight of the opened graves. She'd likely have a poor stomach for that sort of thing. The fainting kind.

Bright color caught his eye. He discovered a pink blanket spread in a shady clearing, a basket that must contain food, and an opaque bottle that offered something to drink.

"Neato! A private picnic."

Owen went back to the field of labor to gather up the fallen woman. The workmen stood as he had left them, mutely staring at the slumped body. They turned their heads to gaze after the pink-clad body as it vanished into the timber and Owen recognized the key to command— all *he* needed was a change of clothing to become the shop steward or the prince of the realm. Well, that and a change of voice.

Owen pulled and hauled and tugged the limp form through the underbrush and finally got it onto the blanket. He was more than a little tired by the struggle, but he made sure that her face wasn't in the sun and that she rested in a comfortable position before he flopped down beside her. She had remarkably long legs. Owen contemplated the legs for a moment and then reached for the lunch basket.

He could almost guess which factory hands had whipped up the meal.

The bread was very good and he could believe that it had been made by either of the two skilled bakers who had worked near him that morning. The meat to accompany the bread was tough and scrawny, poor horse, and Owen thought the man who'd made it must have been a shoemaker in his first life. There was a jar of something gooey that may have been lemon pudding, and then again it may have been yellow glue. He spat it out of his mouth and rinsed the taste with whiskey. The opaque bottle contained a lukewarm liquid that was either limeade or bitter grapefruit juice—the stuff defied identification and Owen put it aside. His own manufactured juice was more palatable. A few apples remained in the bottom of the basket—apples that were rosy red on the outside and inferior pulp inside. He decided that if he hung around this town much longer, eating this kind of scratch, he'd lodge a complaint with somebody.

Owen finished lunch and lit another cigar. It was only marginally better than the first. He'd surely have to do better when he got another chance at the machine—his cigars were as poor as the sandwich meat. Perhaps he'd been too harsh on that shoemaker.

The woman stirred on the blanket beside him and Owen glanced down. She had large brown eyes and they were open, fixed on him. Her face was pale.

"Good morning, cupcake. Feeling better?"

The woman jerked to a sitting position and edged away from him. She was still wobbly and braced both hands on the blanket to keep herself upright. The pale face and brown eyes revealed her alarm.

"Take it easy, honey, I won't bite." Owen gave her a warm smile that was meant to be reassuring. "No rape, no hanky-panky. I'm a respecter of American womanhood and you are a neat one. Indiana boys always *ask* first and say please." He offered the jug. "Try a nip of this. It's recommended for snakebite and fainting spells."

The woman stared at the bottle but kept a distance. She seemed to regard Owen as an apparition.

"I brought you in out of the sun, baby doll. You'd burn to a crisp out there." He examined the pale skin of her face but couldn't decide if that paleness was caused by her faint or was her natural coloring. She had long brown hair to complement the dark brown eyes, but that was no clue to her natural color.

"Now, then," Owen said cheerfully. "Your first question will be: 'Who are you?' And then you'll ask about my equilibrium. Everybody does, so be my guest." He sipped a drink and waited for her reaction.

She only stared at what he was doing.

Owen raised the flap on his breast pocket and invited her to read his number.

"My name is Owen Hall. I'm a new boy here."

Still half afraid of him and ready to bolt or fight if he made the wrong move, the woman reached out timidly and touched his identification bar. Her thumb moved over the message twice while she eyed the whiskey bottle with open wonder. Owen gave her all the time she wanted to read his bug number.

"See? I'm just one of the guys."

With bewilderment she said, "But you spoke to me—are speaking to me."

"I talk to everybody. I'm made that way."

"You are . . . different?"

"In more ways than one, cupcake."

"Do you actually drink the liquid in that bottle?"

"Well, of course! That's what it's for. Eat, drink, and be merry, for tomorrow we go to—to whatever this crazy place is. And anyway, I've already arrived. Here, look here." And he showed the woman her depleted lunch basket. "I helped myself to your picnic goodies, but between you and me, toots, the meat and the pudding should be thrown to the hogs. Somebody didn't have his mind on his business."

The woman inspected the basket with some surprise. "You eat *and* drink!" She seemed to find that incredible.

"Doesn't everybody?"

"No."

"The dumb clucks don't know what they're missing. Those birds out there are losing half the fun of life."

"Were you hiding from me in the excavation?"

"Oh, horsefeathers."

"What were you doing in there?"

"Exploring, finding this ring." Owen reached into his pocket for the topaz treasure. "Pretty, ain't it?"

"Was it yours?" She watched his eyes closely.

"Nope. Never saw it before today, but it's mine now, unless that fella comes around to claim it." He lifted his gaze to hers. "What are you digging up all those stiffs for? Won't the next of kin raise a row about that?"

"The males are reconstituted for the labor force."

"That sounds like slave labor to me. Are you the official grave robber?"

She said, "I am the supervisor of reclamation for this city. It is quite legal. The males are reclaimed and given useful employment. It is a privilege to serve the city."

"Horsefeathers," Owen said again. "You sound like a couple of guys in Europe, names of Hitler and Mussolini. If you live long enough to dig them up, cupcake, you'll

have one hell of a mess on your hands. They don't cooperate worth a tinker's damn."

"I don't know that city. Are they interred?"

"They're still alive and kicking, worse the luck."

The woman peered curiously at his face. "What is that
object in your mouth?"

"A cigar. Want one?"

"Are you eating it?"

"I'm smoking it, you ninny. Use those brown eyes."

"And what is the liquid in the bottle?"

"Whiskey, rotgut. Want a nip?"

"What does whiskey rotgut do?"

"It makes me glow in the dark."

"Where did you obtain the cigar and the whiskey?"

"From the big machine, of course. Where else?"

"Was there no objection?"

"Nobody said a word," Owen assured her.

She studied him in speculative silence for a while and
Owen thought she was letting her guard down. The early
fright of him was passing; tension and apprehension were
slowly fading, leaving only wonderment. Owen guessed
that not many people wandered by to inspect her dig-
gings.

At length she asked quietly, "Are you a variant?"

"I don't know. What's a variant?"

"A male who has been reconstituted in a different manner for a different purpose. One who is not given useful
employment in the factories."

He considered that. "A particular purpose?"

"A very particular purpose." Her voice dropped.

"Ah, you mean something special." He mulled that. "I
suppose so—I guess so. I'm not like the other nitwits
around here. I'm different from those guys digging the
graves out yonder. I'm different from all those other guys
I met on the road this morning. I *know* what I'm doing."

She was insistent. "A variant is designed for a very
specific purpose." Again her voice carried a meaning.

"Nothing illegal, I hope."

"Certainly not! The practice isn't common, but it is
quite legal. It wouldn't be done otherwise, for the good of
the city." She bent forward and peered into his eyes, attempting to read secrets there. "Was there . . . was there
a particular woman last night or this morning? An unusual woman?" Her manner had subtly changed.

"Hah! There sure as hell was, and I'm not apt to forget her! Honey, when I left home and hit the road this morning, *that* hellcat was spinning her wheels. Looped. She couldn't stand up straight. Oh, boy—she'd had it!"

"Do you mean she was ill?"

"No. I mean she was flying, floating, jumping with the old joy juice. She took on more than she could handle in one night. You know, three sheets in the wind."

"I am not familiar with that expression."

Owen fluttered his hands. "She was out of her head—Up, high, blotto, crazy, loaded with joy juice. I don't think I've *ever* seen a woman that high before."

"She was exhilarated? Enraptured?"

"And how! She was going off in all directions."

The brown-eyed woman stared at him with wonder and commented, "Oh." Her attitude toward Owen was shifting and now she seemed at once both fascinated and repelled.

"She won't forget last night in a hurry," Owen said.

"May I assume that she liked it?"

He grinned at the memory. "You can say that again. Cupcake, I think it was her first time, and she didn't know how to handle it. Just overwhelmed by it all, I guess." He tapped his chest with a finger. "Now me—I'm an old hand at the game. I know when to indulge and when to quit, but *that* baby took on quite a load."

She said once again, "Oh."

Owen relit his cigar and wondered if he had enough matches to last the day. The brown-eyed cupcake was good company and he just might decide to spend the afternoon with her; it was obvious that she was becoming attracted to him, now that she'd gotten over her fright.

The woman studied him with open curiosity, finding a new facet to his nature that was foreign to hers. She was fascinated by a discovery.

"You *are* a variant," she said after a lengthy study. "I have not seen one before. You possess certain skills and privileges not given to other males."

Owen thought he could agree with that. "There ain't no flies on me."

"What are you doing here?"

"Collecting horsefeathers."

"What are horsefeathers?"

"The rarest kind in all this world, cupcake. You don't come across them very often."

"Have you found any?"

"Not yet, but I've got all day."

"Who assigned you to that task?"

"I don't know her name—we were busy with something else." Owen dug into his pocket for the metallic card the blonde had given him. He ran his thumb over the plate and passed it to the woman. "No name—just nothing but numbers here."

Her eyes widened as she read first the identification and then the address. The woman stared at Owen with a new astonishment. It was a day of startling discoveries.

"Paoli!"

"You know her—really know her? Is that her name? Well, neato! She never *did* get around to telling me her name—I guess I kept her pretty busy, what with one thing and other, and she didn't think of it." Owen reframed an image in his mind. "A tall blonde dolly with a freckle on the tip of her nose. I'll bet she bats a thousand."

"Paoli." The woman's brown eyes had grown very large and she inspected Owen anew. "Are you going there again tonight?"

"And how! Honey, I was *ordered* to be there tonight, and I wouldn't miss the party for anything. We're going to cut a rug."

"What does that mean?"

"We're going to peel the apple, celebrate, jump. I'm going to show her what Indiana boys can do in ragtime."

Hesitantly: "Do you . . . do you please her?"

Owen waggled the calling card before the very large brown eyes and then put it away. "How do you think I got this, by picking her pocket? She said, *'Be there,'* and, cupcake, I'm going to *be there* with bells on. She said she wanted to learn more about me, how I operate—you know—she wants to tinker around with one thing and another."

With awe: "You actually . . . touched Paoli?"

"Well, I didn't shine her shoes." He looked at her chest. "We played push the button. Want me to show you what I did?" His hands drifted toward her identification.

"No, *no*." The woman actually shrank away from him. "That will not be necessary."

"My loss," Owen assured her. "I won't get to know you." He thought he saw a blush on her face, but it may have been only her natural color returning. He offered the bottle again. "Sure you wouldn't care for a nip?"

"I don't drink wine."

"It's not wine, it's whiskey—the best the machine and me could make. I'd be pleased to teach you the difference."

Firmly: "No."

"Whatever you say, cupcake. But I'll admit that I'm disappointed. You and me could have one bang-up blanket party right here in the woods, and there'd be no trouble from them zombies out there." Owen relaxed on the blanket, stretching out his legs to those corners not already occupied by the woman. "What's your name?"

"Kehli."

"You don't look Irish, but I'll take your word for it." He took another swallow and set the bottle aside. "I'm going to rest up a bit, Kelly; I've had a busy day and I know I'll have a busy night. War or no war, there's going to be a hot time in that old town tonight. If you get lonely you're welcome to come over and join our party." He saw the expression on her face, misread it, and added, "Oh, Paoli won't mind. I'll tell her I invited you."

"I think not. No."

"Maybe you'll change your mind when you see me in action. Us ol' Indiana boys have a pretty good reputation at cutting rugs." Owen squinted up through the treetops at the sunlight and closed his eyes for a nap. "Wake me up if you want *anything*, cupcake."

Kehli made no answer.

She had pulled away to one corner of the blanket when he had stretched out and now she doubled her legs to her chest, hugging her knees to her chin and watching the variant. The timber was wholly silent. After a while the woman reached for an apple and ate it slowly, never abandoning her study of the sleeping male. The fascination would not fade. She wondered if it would be exciting to have her own variant, and if so—would *she* wake up in the morning to find herself looped and blotto. Was blotto fun?

Once, when she was very sure the variant was asleep, she cautiously touched his chest. It felt firm.

Owen would have given a penny or two for her thoughts had he been awake.

Kehli was gone from the blanket.

Owen sat up sleepily, rubbed his eyes, discovered the picnic basket beside him, and realized that the lady hadn't deserted him. She was probably in the cemetery, supervising the digs. He pocketed the whiskey bottle—after sampling the contents to make sure the quality hadn't deteriorated while he slept—and got to his feet to search for her.

The crew was preparing to leave the field.

They stood in a ragged line, each with a mummy case balanced on one shoulder and awaiting the word to march. One man was gathering up the tools of the trade and stacking them alongside an unopened grave, the target for tomorrow. When that man was finished with the task, he scooped up a coffin and took his place at the end of the line.

Kehli was satisfied with the tidying detail and turned to discover Owen standing there watching her.

"You're quitting early," he said. His own shadow was about his feet. "It can't be past noon."

"We have our daily quota."

"I like the hours around this here town. The factory quit a long time ago."

"Something must have gone wrong. They usually work until late afternoon." She hesitated and then asked curiously, "What will you do now?"

"Guess I'll go back to town with you," Owen said. He pointed a finger at the waiting line. "I've never seen one man carrying a coffin before."

"The contents are not heavy. Go get the—Will you bring the blanket and the basket?"

"Chop-chop."

He folded the pink blanket into a neat square, hung the basket over his arm, and went back to join the waiting line. Kehli stood at the head of the column and Owen fell in immediately behind her, elbowing a zombie aside. The zombie made no protest. The woman called out the marching order and the workmen obediently followed her and Owen. They retraced a path through the weedy grasses that had been trampled down by several previous passages between city and cemetery.

Owen looked around her shoulder at the buildings and the rolling road, heat-hazy in the distance.

"What's the name of this here town?"

"Thirty-four. The Mother's Thirty-fourth city."

"Never heard of it. Is it in Indiana?"

"What is Indiana?"

"That means it's not in Indiana," Owen said gloomily. "I sure as hell wish I knew where I was—am. Have you ever heard of heaven or hell?"

"I don't know those cities."

"That's what I thought." He watched the backsides of the pink coveralls plodding along before him. "Who's Mother?"

"Mother is *Mother*. The sovereign."

"That means the Queen Bee," Owen said. "Dig, dig, dig, make bread and bacon and eggs for the Queen Bee and her brood. Some life—I don't think. How am I going to find out what happened to Indiana?" He watched her brown hair dangling over the neckline of the pink coveralls. "Don't you know there's a war on? We just say DYKTAWO?"

"I know of no war."

"Well, there *is*," he insisted. "Even Lucky Strike Green has gone to war. We've got food and gasoline rationing, and wage and price controls, and everybody's saving up copper and aluminum to help the war effort. If you have any money left over—which ain't likely—you buy war bonds. Some of the guys I work with are chewing cut plug because they can't get any cigarettes except Ramses, and nobody in their right minds will smoke Ramses. I don't have problems with my cigars, though. There ain't no shortage of cigars or cut plug. We got Cuba on our side."

"I have not heard of this."

"Actually, there's two wars on all at the same time— one in Europe and the other in the South Pacific—but we ain't winning either one of them, hardly. We seem to be getting whupped all along the line. The Nazis are spread out all over Europe and parts of Africa, and now they're into Russia too. I *think* Russia is in Europe, somewhere. It's pretty bad, let me tell you. Well, not *all* that bad. The Russians are pretty good fighters—they stopped the Nazi Sixth Army at a town called Stalingrad, stopped them cold and beat them to a frazzle. The Sixth Army surrendered about a month ago, but that's the only place

I know of where our side is winning. I guess we're losing just everywhere else. Something good has *got* to happen soon."

"I don't know those cities."

"We already lost the Philippines and MacArthur had to run for it—he escaped in a submarine and wound up in Australia, saying he'd be back. Well, maybe he will, but I wouldn't bet on it. And we lost Bataan and Corregidor and all those places over there, and the British lost Singapore. That's not in Europe, you understand, that's the other way." He waved the cigar in desolate fashion. "All the news the last couple of years is pretty bad. Lose, lose, lose all the damned time. I'd sure like to know what else has happened since . . . since I was twenty-eight. You're not much help, cupcake."

"I know none of those cities—they are not in the Mother's sovereignty. There is no war—all the cities live in peace. Your variance has produced an awkward mixture of mind."

"You think I'm crazy?"

"I accept that you are a variant, I accept that you were reconstituted for a purpose other than manual labor, but I don't understand your thought processes and speech patterns and so I am led to suspect that your reconstitution was imperfect. There was some error in reclamation, which would be my fault, or an error in your restoration." She turned to give him a troubled glance. "The other males do not speak of cities or war—they appear to have no memories and do not speak at all unless they are questioned."

"Paoli said that. She said I was incomplete."

"I agree with her. Your mind is as strange as your behavior. You appear to be living in a past life."

"One of us is crazy," Owen muttered. He fished the bottle from his pocket and took a swallow to demonstrate that *he* wasn't crazy. A man could make a pretty good case for sanity around this town; a man could point his finger at the emptied graves and ask who was sane and who wasn't.

"Do you want to know what I think, cupcake?"

"I am unable to follow your thought patterns."

"You already said that, but I'll tell you anyway. I think we lost—lost the war. I think we got skunked. I think the Germans and the Italians and the Japanese won and

they own the *whole* world now. They put you in charge
to run the place for them, that's what I think. You're
serving the enemy."

"I serve only the city."

"Are you a WAAC?"

"What does that mean?"

"The Women's Army Auxiliary Corps, of course. The
President and the generals put their heads together last
year and created a female army—all women and girls.
They wear the same uniform and everything. Well, they
don't fight in the trenches, but they back up the boys on
the home front. I saw some of them in Saint Louis last
fall. They were neat."

"I serve only the city and supervise reclamation. There
is no female army."

"I still say there's something fishy about this place,
Kelly. How long was I dead down there?"

"I am not able to answer that."

"I figure five or six months—say, from February to
August." The hot sun made him certain of August.

"Surely that isn't correct."

"Well, then, how old are you? Right now, today?"

"I am thirty years."

"Is that so?" He surveyed the figure before him and
pursed his lips, nearly dropping the cigar. "Not bad for
your age, not bad at all. Me, I'm twenty eight, if you
want to wait for me. Been earning my own living since I
was fifteen—I rode a bicycle, I was a printer's devil and
delivery boy for the town's newspaper and job shop.
Have you been around here since you were born?"

"I was born in the city I serve."

"Really born? Not just dug up?"

"Only the male work force is reclaimed."

"How long has the city been there?"

"Always."

"I doubt that." Owen cast about for a way to get
through to the woman and remembered a code number
on the identification bar worn by the blonde traffic warden. "Hey, Kelly! What does *b08-136* mean on a bar?"

The woman glanced around again. "Was that Paoli?
It signifies that she was born in the eight month of the
hundred and thirty-sixth year. Was that really Paoli?"

"That was really Paoli. She let me know everything,
the works. Now then, cupcake, let's get down to the

brass base: the hundred and thirty-sixth year of what?"

Kehli said with satisfaction, "I am three years the younger."

"Bully for you. The hundred and thirty-sixth year of *what?*"

"Of the Mother's sovereignty."

"She is a hundred and thirty-six years old?"

"That is absurd. There was a Mother before her, and a Mother, and a Mother, and a—"

"Knock it off!" Owen cried. "I'm sorry I asked. What you're trying to say is, your history is a hundred and thirty-six years long *and* thirty-three more if Paoli is just that old now. All told, a hundred and sixty-nine years right up to today. Are you reading me?"

"I am not looking at you. I cannot read you if I am not looking at you and touching your identification."

"If I wasn't an Indiana gentleman, I'd say a dirty word right *here.*" Owen reached out to grasp her shoulder, knowing the unfamiliar touch would provoke a reaction. The woman stopped walking and spun around. Owen stopped and waited while the zombie line behind collided with him and then eased away without being told.

"You touched me!"

"I touched you, cupcake. Now, please listen carefully with both ears. *Has* somebody's mother been the Queen Bee here for a hundred and sixty-nine years? Is that the length of your history—your town?"

"That is correct."

He pointed past her arm. "The town isn't *that* old. The road isn't *that* old."

"The city and the road are continually being rebuilt. They must endure." She turned about and gave an order to the workmen. The homeward march continued.

Owen mulled the information but found that it gave him little satisfaction. If he believed her, if she was right, it meant that he had met up with the Pennsy freight train something more than 169 years ago. It meant that what he'd thought was an instantaneous reawakening was not so instantaneous after all; there had been an intermission between the acts lasting more than a century and a half. Incredible. It meant that *this* place was the only promised land to be had and that he'd hung around in a never-never nowhere for more than a 169 years waiting for Kehli to dig him up and for a drunken broad to put him back together again in the wrong way. It meant—

Owen cried, "Balderdash!"

"What?"

"I don't believe it, none of it. This isn't Indiana. Maybe you've been knocking around here for a hundred and sixty-nine years taking care of Mother and rebuilding the city and all, but *this* isn't Indiana, and there's still a war going on out there somewhere." He swept his hand over the great prairie. "Wherever *somewhere* is. I've got to go out there and find Indiana again—I've got to find the United States real soon now!"

"I really don't understand your thought processes."

"*Yours* ain't all that easy, cupcake."

Owen trudged along behind the woman, puzzling it. The scene failed to make sense no matter how he twisted or squeezed it. He was certain this was not his home state, and the summer heat wouldn't let him believe it was February 1943. That much was acceptable; that much could be taken as gospel. A tiny little gap in months *did* exist between *that* February and *this* August, and he *had* met a freight train at a crossing and suddenly stopped being twenty-eight years old. That could be added to the gospel. But next—but next he was alive again and bouncing around *this* place where nobody had ever heard of Indiana, and some people were telling him that he was fitted together wrong. Balderdash.

Kehli stopped so quickly that Owen bumped into her. They had arrived at the edge of the rolling road. The zombies bunched up behind Owen, crowding him.

"Back off, or I'll punch your snoot!"

Kehli was peering down the road, a hand to her eyes.

Owen asked, "What's going on down there?"

"There appears to be something amiss."

Owen crushed the cigar under his foot and squinted into the distance. Something amiss—and he thought he could guess what. Five traffic wardens were working the road toward the southwest, working with their backs to Owen and Kehli but being slowly carried toward them. The wardens were checking every male on the roadway, reading their identifications and staring closely into dull eyes. They advanced like a living pink wall, five bodies wide, and no workman escaped their scrutiny. Here a man received a thump on the chest to provoke a reaction and there another had fingers snapped just above the ridge of his nose. The inspection was prolonged and thorough, missing nothing by not being hurried.

"Trouble?" Owen asked again.

"Perhaps there has been a disturbance, or a subversion of order. They are seeking a specific individual. It is unusual for so many males to be on the road this early in the day."

"Maybe the factories are closed."

"They should not be."

"Tell you what, cupcake," Owen said judiciously. "I think somebody's called a strike. The natives are revolting."

Six

Peace and rest at length have come,
All the day's long toil is past;
And each heart is whispering,
"Home, Home at last!"

      —Thomas Hood

Owen Hall thought he may as well play the zombie—he was in good company, and protective coloration was suddenly the order of the day.

The inquisitive wardens working the road didn't appear to have a sense of humor—they were too intent upon turning up some miscreant. (Perhaps some factory worker had taken home a machine to make bacon for himself.) When the moving road brought the investigators near he dropped his gaze and stared fixedly at Kehli's pink posterior. He missed any visual byplay, but he heard the exchange between Kehli and the nearest warden. That woman had turned as the road brought her abreast the waiting group.

"Are you responsible for this crew?"

Kehli said, "I am. This is the reclamation crew."

Owen thought that should have been obvious. They weren't using the coffins to smuggle in black market butter.

"How long have you been in the field?"

"Since the call, just after sunrise."

"They haven't returned to the city in the meantime?"

"No, not until now."

There was a long moment of speculative silence and Owen *knew* he was being scrutinized. He held his body stiff and kept his gaze on Kehli's rump. The blanket was on one arm and her picnic basket hung from the other. Owen's vivid imagination said that if the inquisitorial warden had a truncheon, she would now be fingering it with loving care while she searched for a likely spot on his skull.

There was a fink loose in the town. Somebody had snitched on him. The drunken broad, or Paoli, or the gray old woman at the factory had snitched on him and now he was a wanted man. Maybe, just maybe, the wardens had beat a confession from that hellion behind the green door. Or maybe that succulent cucumber had already turned up on someone's lunch plate. They had his bug number.

When the warden's voice was heard again, it was a short distance away. The road had carried her past them.

"Very well. Thank you for your courtesy."

"Thank you," Kehli replied, and gave an order to the crew to mount the road.

A good old Indiana cop would have had apoplexy after hearing that polite exchange.

Owen climbed aboard and very nearly betrayed himself, very nearly turned to help Kehli on board. Some one of the wardens down the road would be watching. He busied himself with the mummy cases because that seemed safe enough; he pulled while those on the ground shoved the cases onto the roadway. Kehli climbed up unassisted.

They began the distribution of the spoils.

The woman had a list of numbers and one of the cases was dropped off each time they reached a door with a corresponding number. NO-770 got a delivery, and the entire crew left the road to watch lest they be carried away while Kehli and a zombie made the drop. There was no ceremony. Kehli made a clicking noise with her tongue and pointed. The crew understood the signals. The workman standing next to her stepped off the road and placed his burden on the doorstep, putting it crosswise so that the occupant of the house couldn't enter or leave without falling over the obstacle. Kehli checked off a number on her list, clicked again, and made a little gesture. The crew returned to the rolling road and rode on to the next drop number.

Owen thought it was like Father Christmas making his rounds in August and acknowledged that the delivery system showed organization even though the gifts left something to be desired. Most red-blooded Indiana girls would prefer mink coats or diamonds or a ten-pound sack of sugar.

Owen also noted that Kehli's back was to him most of the time—she seemed to have forgotten his presence while she carried out her duties. After the third coffin had been deposited on the third doorstep, he had a new bug number. The worker standing behind him hadn't so much as batted his eyes when Owen deftly switched their identification bars. He was now *Recla/H-26034-28* and no question mark. It was pleasing to be twenty-eight again. Owen muttered his thanks to the donor.

When the distribution was complete Kehli ordered the workmen to go home and to return to the cemetery tomorrow. The zombies separated and rode away.

Owen first made sure there were no wardens watching, then handed over the blanket and picnic basket.

"It's been nice, cupcake. I had a good day."

She studied him for a long moment. "What will you do now?"

"Go home, I reckon. Could be there's something hot on the stove for me." He looked up into her friendly eyes. "Unless you'd like me to come over to your place *first*. Got anything in mind?"

"No," she said too quickly. "No."

He patted the bottle in his pocket. "I've got enough to go around."

"No." She appeared to be blushing again.

"Suit yourself." He dug out the address card and thumb-read the final numbers. "I've got to find B-343. It's away back yonder somewhere on the other side of the timber. I'll have to ride all the way around town."

Kehli said, "I also live in B section. Paoli is a neighbor."

"Well, good! Remember what I said about the party tonight—if you're lonely and want to find out how Indiana boys peel the apple, come on over. Want a nip before you go? Last chance, now. Say—where *are* you going?"

"That does not concern—" She stopped and began again. "I am not accustomed to being questioned. I must submit today's reclamation list to the registrar and draw a new list for tomorrow."

"Back to the office, and dig, dig, dig." Owen nodded. "You people are in the same old rut. Okay, cupcake, suit yourself. I'm going home. Don't forget my invitation if you get thirsty or lonely. I've got something here to take your mind off your work."

The inquisitive and still fascinated woman asked one more question before they parted near a building that resembled the factory of Owen's early-morning experience.

"Are all variants like you?"

"Damifino. I'm the only variant I've ever met. Try one sometime and find out for yourself."

She stepped off the road and left him, wearing an expression that Owen thought he could read. It would be a pleasure. He knew better than to look back, although he wanted to turn and wave goodbye, blow a kiss, or something to express his appreciation. Kehli was nice. The several hours spent in her company had been the most pleasant hours of the day—and he'd be willing to spend the night as well if he didn't already have a date.

The road carried him around the city.

Twice he was examined by wardens before he reached the door that was his destination. He had been riding with his eyes cast down, mulling the events of the day, and hadn't seen the first inquisitor until the flash of pink appeared before him and a hand plucked at the flap of his breast pocket. Owen stood passive and let the woman read his new number. She seemed satisfied and went on her way. The second warden accosted him on the opposite side of town, when he was nearing the house he sought. She read his bar, thumped his chest to learn if he would respond, then read the number a second time and left him alone.

Owen told himself he was a hunted outlaw, destined for the salt mines if they learned his true identity. Somebody had snitched and now they were hunting him down.

He was surprised to discover that number B-343 had a green door. It was not the sickly green door he'd been thrown through in the early-morning hours but instead a soothing pastel green that he imagined fitted Paoli's personality. There was another door of bilious green just three or four houses up the road, toward that distant timber, and yet another one of indeterminate greenish hue a few houses behind him, but B-343 was a pleasing pastel he could live with. Owen swung off the road and went up the narrow walkway to knock loudly on the door.

There was no response.

He knocked again, then turned the knob and pushed, but the door refused to admit him. He put more strength into a second attempt, but the panel held fast to its latch.

Owen kicked it open and stepped into the darkened interior. The remains of the door entered with him.

"Hi, honey, I'm home!"

Honey failed to reply.

A few shattered bits of the door clung to the hinges but most of the debris was at his feet. It had been a most shoddily constructed door; an apprentice carpenter could have done better. Ordinary plate hinges on the outside of the frame had held the door—any burglar with a screwdriver could enter after a few minutes' work.

The house was scarcely a house in the familiar sense, despite exterior appearances. In one way it reminded Owen of the factory, and in another it suggested a skinny tapering apartment. The house—or the apartment —consisted of one very long room stretching from front door to back door, having room dividers set here and there to break the vast monotonous expanse of the whole. The room was appreciably narrower at the rear. There were no windows in the room, no pretty pictures on the walls, no carpets on the floor, and no useless but ornamental bric-a-brac scattered about to catch dust. A dismal place.

The dividers were opaque screens mounted on small casters for mobility. Between those dividers Owen found a spartan lounge area, a dining area, the blonde's bedroom, a cubbyhole alongside the bedroom that served as a bath, and at the very rear of the long room another divider that concealed a cot. A bare cot, but nothing more —nary a pillow, blanket, nor chamber pot. Owen stared at the cot and shook his head—be damned if he'd sleep on *that*.

The remainder of the apartment was a workshop, and here the suggestion of a factory was too broad to be ignored. It *was* a factory, dominated by a replica of the machine. A think-and-do machine just like downtown, but smaller, of course. The curved bar for the forehead, the window, and the row of buttons were set higher off the floor, tailored for the female occupant of the place rather than the peasants. The only other discernible difference in design was that *this* machine had a delivery door on one side—an opening that exactly resembled an oven door. It was a man-sized opening, not like the small cleanout door he'd used to recover his whiskey and cigars.

Owen pulled the door open to peek inside. The oven was empty but for a smidgen of dust and an odor that caused him to wrinkle his nose and slam the door.

One of the streamlined mummy cases lay on the floor alongside the machine near the oven door. Because he was nosy, Owen lifted the lid of the coffin and looked inside. He closed it fast and backed away.

A long workbench claimed his attention. It was a cluttered bench—the sign of a busy practitioner.

A large-sized and well-worn book caught his eye and he picked it up to thumb the pages. Owen guessed it to be a service manual, a handy volume delivered with every home machine together with a ninety-day warranty. Several of the early pages folded out to double spreads and reminded him of blueprints, or schematic drawings, or something like that. The text was written in a peculiar English he failed to grasp and the technical terms were not at all familiar to a journeyman carpenter. What did an educated Indiana boy know—or need to know—about a clavicle, a sacrum, a patella? The illustrations were remarkably clear and comprehensible. They depicted men —sort of.

Owen slammed the book shut, suddenly ill at ease. His stomach threatened an uprising. He didn't like to look at skeletons and at livid manlike things with their skins off. It was positively indecent.

There were several hand tools on the bench—some familiar and some not—as well as a large box that contained two pairs of dun-colored coveralls and two pairs of work shoes. The garments weren't as well made, or as stylish, as the several pairs of pink coveralls hanging in the bedroom. Owen thought that if he put his mind to it, he could whip up some pretty snappy clothes for himself in the think-and-do machine—especially if he had a copy of the Sears catalogue as a reference. For that matter, he could get the blonde out of her coveralls and into a dress, although doing up a pair of silk stockings and high-heeled pumps would tax his faculties somewhat.

Owen discovered a jar of old coins tucked away behind the box and was in the act of removing the lid to examine the treasure when he heard a noise at the door. He put down the jar and went to investigate.

The lady of the house was home.

He said in greeting, "Hi, there, toots. Nice little place you've got here." But that was a white lie.

The lady of the house was staring with consternation at the shattered remains of the door. Her surprise on seeing him in the house was equaled by her dismay at the wreckage. One hand was sweeping back and forth in the open doorway as if groping for the missing panel. The hand struck a fragment of wood clinging to the upper hinge, and that fragment fell to the floor.

She cried, "What are you doing in there?"

"Unfair! Unfair!" Owen retorted with heat. *"You* invited me! Now don't try to wiggle out of it—you invited me to come spend the night."

Aghast: "But what happened to this door?"

"I kicked it open. It fell down."

"Why . . . *why* did you do that?"

"Because it was locked," Owen said simply.

"You *can't* kick down doors!"

"I can—I'm an Indiana Democrat."

She stared at him. "Are you looped?"

"Not yet, honey, not yet—but hoo boy! have I got a head start on you. We had a little party this morning."

"We don't have parties at the workshops. Why did you leave your job?"

"That old woman—you know, the granny—stopped the works and sent everybody home. I thought it was a short shift, better than union hours."

"But why did she do that?"

Owen shrugged. "I didn't ask. I'm not a company man."

"Was there a breakdown? Was there a malfunction?"

"Nope. Everything was humming. But if you want a piece of advice, you won't have butter on your toast in the morning. It looked like sick axle grease."

"That is very unusual. *Something* must have gone amiss. There was no explanation?"

"Hah! That old grouch wouldn't explain how to put out a fire."

The frustrated warden looked past him into the interior of the house. "What were you doing in there?"

"Casing the joint. It's a square layout."

"But it *isn't* square," she contradicted him. "It is a trapezoid. Our city is planned."

Owen shook his head with mock sadness. "Honey, do you have any idea what a dumb broad is?"

"No."

"I didn't think so." He waved her forward and held out a helping hand. "You may as well hop over that kindling and come on in. If you stay out there gabbing all day, people will think you're selling subscriptions or something." He moved backward to make way, noting that she avoided his hand. "And stop worrying about your door. I'm a carpenter. I'll hang another one for you—and guarantee it, too."

"How do you know you are a carpenter?"

"I found out things about me today. I've been busy." He patted the twin surprises in his pockets and waited for the right time to introduce the bottles.

The blonde stepped over the wreckage and entered her dwelling in something of a daze. Homecoming was never like this. She scanned the interior to see if anything else had been damaged and then looked back to Owen. Her expression was not one of relief.

"I don't understand you at *all*. You are unlike any other male I've ever known. You are incomprehensible."

"I'm a variant," Owen said proudly, but humbly. It befitted an Indiana variant to be humble upon occasion.

The woman pounced. "How do you know that?"

"I was told so—a nice little brown-eyed doll told me. She dug me, if you get the joke."

The blonde traffic warden studied him in thoughtful silence. At length: "Was there a particular woman last night? Was there an unusual occurrence?"

"Aha!" Owen cried with triumph. "I knew that was coming, I just knew it!" He smacked his fist into a palm. "Yes, there was, and I'm *not* going back there again, no matter what. I don't like what happened and I wouldn't go back there even if I could find the place. No, thanks!"

"You didn't tell me you were a variant this morning."
She made it sound like an accusation.

"I didn't know I *was* a variant this morning, but I've
picked up some smarts since then. We had a picnic, and
I found out one thing and another."

"Who had a picnic?"

"Me and a jolly cupcake named Kelly. She's nice.
A little green, mind you, a little on the dumb side, but
nice. If she listens to me she'll come along fast."

The woman's eyes widened, either with recognition or
in astonishment. "There was *another* woman today?"

"Yep," Owen admitted. "We had a good time out there
in the woods, poking into this and that. She had poor
apples, though. I've seen better."

"Two women? Are you programmed?"

"Good ol' Indiana boys can dance all night. Five, ten
women—it makes no difference. We please 'em all but
we don't bother with programs."

With complete frustration: "I don't understand you!"

"That puts the two of us in the same boat," he retorted.
"What did you do with Indiana?"

"I never had your Indiana. I don't know it."

"Indiana was the place I lived in back there, when I
was twenty-eight the first time. You moved it—you hid
it. And now here we are in one hundred and sixty-nine
and I can't find it."

Incredulously: "How did you know *that?*"

"Easy—I'm a math genius; I know all about Einstein."
He pointed a finger. *"You* were born in one hundred and
thirty-six and you're thirty-three years old. Happy birthday, Paoli."

She stared at him with her mouth half open. It was a
day of astonishments. *"How* did you learn my name?"

Owen tapped his head with an index finger. "Kidneys.
The question is, one hundred and sixty-nine what?"

"What do you mean by what?"

"There you are!" he shouted. "Always trying to give
me the go-by! *What* is B.C. or A.D., or something like
that."

"But what is B.C.A.D.?"

Owen muttered a word that Indiana gentlemen didn't
usually mention in mixed company, but in this instance it
precisely mirrored his frame of mind. The woman was
being obstinate.

Paoli said, "I *wish* I knew your fabricator. You are flawed beyond belief."

"The pot is calling the kettle black again. Honey, you're not all that great yourself, if you know what I mean—which I doubt. I've met a lot of people in this here town who were behind the door when the brains were passed out. The point is, what are we going to do about it?"

"Do about what?"

Owen said dispiritedly, "Geez." He seized her hand and pulled her into the workshop. As before, she was startled by his bold action but she went along with him. Owen paused beside the think-and-do machine and pointed dramatically to the coffin resting on the floor alongside the oven door.

"Poor old Yorick is stuffed in there, in that box. Shame on you!"

Incredulously: "Did you know him?"

"Never saw him before in my life—either of my lives. Do you specialize in reconstituted orange juice?" He stood almost against her and peered up into her eyes in the same investigatory manner used by the wardens. His index finger tapped her chest. "I've got your number, babe."

"But of course you have. I gave it to you this morning." She stared down at the finger on her chest.

"Not that number, dammit!" Owen cried. "I mean, I *know* what's going on here, in this house, in this town. I know everything! I know all about them zombies out there and where you're getting them. Those guys are retreads!"

Paoli looked down at Owen for a long while as his shouting died away and silence returned to the house. At last she said, "You are flawed. I am sorry about that, but the flaw must be eradicated." Each word was given careful enunciation to make it fully understood. She held the close inspection of him.

The long silence was unnerving.

Owen shifted uncomfortably under her stare and looked away, looked around the long room seeking a distraction. He took a backward step to put safe distance between them and sought to turn her attention. He felt like a microbe under a microscope, and he wasn't at all anxious to hop into anybody's oven to be rebuilt.

The jar of old coins caught his eye; now *there* was a handful of clues to the mystery of the missing States.

Owen darted over to the workbench. He twisted the lid off the jar and spilled the coins out onto the bench. A few of them were burnished, suggesting that she had tried to clean them, but the others were black and pitted.

"Hey, come here—look at these things." He waved imperiously. "Where did you get these?"

She followed Owen to the bench, watching him closely. "The objects turn up occasionally during our excavations. The ancient peoples used them in their religious ceremonies. They are called monies."

"I *know* what they are—I'm an ancient people." He turned over a dime. "Just look at this date."

Owen sorted the coins. There was a solitary penny, several dimes, a few quarters, a half-dollar, and two other coins that were wholly unknown to him. The penny was dated 1940 and Owen grunted his satisfaction at the familiar date. That was close to home; that was only a bit more than two years ago, just before the war. Two of the dimes were of the Mercury coinage and bore the dates 1915 and 1943. The remainder were later Roosevelt dimes, and Owen inspected them with an eager fascination. It was strange—eerie—to find his own President portrayed on the coins; perhaps they had put his likeness there because he was the first man in history to serve three terms in the White House.

Owen was filled with a sense of wonder. The two Mercury dimes were put carefully aside.

The quarters were of minimal interest because all the dates were common and quite familiar to him; they ranged from 1920 through 1941. The half-dollar was something else again and earned a prolonged scrutiny: 1984. Owen stared with disfavor at the man's profile stamped on the coin and muttered an indistinct vilification. Imagine *that* jackass winding up famous, with his picture on a fifty-cent piece!

Owen hunched over the two remaining mystery coins.

"Look at these things," he demanded of Paoli. "Just look: *ten shul.* Now, what in hell is ten shul? It was made in two thousand ninety-seven by something called the NorAmerFed. What do you know about the NorAmerFed? Does that mean the North American Federation?"

She moved in beside him. "I have heard something of it in my childhood. A myth, really—a Mother's story told to children at bedtime. It is said that NorAmer-Fed was a most ancient land, a kingdom now lost in antiquity; it is said that the land was the prized possession of a mythical male deity. In those days the male gods owned everything and gave cities as gifts to their favorite sons. The gods and their sons rode across the sky on obedient clouds." Paoli was sympathetic. "I know no more than that, and I trust I have not offended you and your gods. Do you have knowledge of the ancients?"

"I know all about the United States, but I never heard of this fool thing," Owen said.

"I thought the name was familiar to you."

"Baby doll, you need a geography lesson. Indiana is *in* the United States, and the United States is *in* North America. North America is the name of this here continent; I guess it covers everything from the North Pole to the Panama Canal." He tapped the strange coins. "But I never heard of the NorAmerFed, I never heard of ten shul, and I never saw two thousand ninety-seven in all my life. Even my grandchildren never saw two thousand ninety-seven, if I had any grandchildren, which I don't, but you know what I mean. What in hell happened to Indiana and the United States after I died?"

"I cannot know that. I am sorry for you."

Owen pushed the two coins across the bench to Paoli. "They made these shuls in two thousand eighty-one and two thousand ninety-seven. Boy! Talk about that crazy Buck Rogers stuff!"

"Was he an ancient god who rode in the sky?"

Owen muttered under his breath, but failed to reply. He turned his somber attention to the two Mercury dimes, flipping them over to read the mint marks and rolling them between his fingers. They had the good old feel of home: he might have actually owned one dime or the other at some time; he might have spent them at Ollie Cronin's drugstore or at Juanita's Grocery just down the street.

He gave the dimes to the attentive woman. "Here, read them."

"Read what?" It wasn't what she had expected.

"Read the dates."

"One nine one five. Is that significant?"

"It sure as hell is, honeybun. That's the year I was born; nineteen fifteen. Not dug up, not reconstituted, but *born*." He indicated the other coin. "Now read that one."

"One nine four three." She waited expectantly.

"Yep, nineteen forty-three. The year I stopped being twenty-eight. I never even made it to the opening game that year."

The woman was sympathetic. "I realize that you consider it a most solemn and historic date."

Owen nodded agreement, knowing a sudden melancholy mood. "Well, it gives a guy a funny feeling in the pit of his stomach. Two dimes, twenty cents, and one marks the beginning while the other signifies the end. And they turn up here, of all places. It makes a guy think."

She asked softly, "Do you wish me to withdraw?"

"Withdraw? What for?"

"You might wish to pray privately."

Owen nearly hurled the coins across the workshop. "You don't pray on them, dimwit, you spend them!"

"How do you spend them?"

"On beer—when you can find dime beer anymore. The last time I was in Hartford City the bandits wanted fifteen cents a glass. Can you picture that? They're taking advantage of honest workingmen just because there's a war on. I hope somebody reports them to the Price Control Board."

"What is beer?"

"Pale booze. Oh—" Owen remembered the jugs in his pockets and brought them out for display. "This stuff. I call it Owen's Choice." He removed the cap from a bottle and generously sampled the contents. "Now, *that's* smooth. It will tickle your toenails, baby doll."

She looked at the bottles with a new and sudden interest. "I hesitate to ask where you found them; your answers are unintelligible. I know the term *booze* now—I researched the subject in the files this morning."

"Bully for you. What did you find out?"

" 'Booze' was the name of one of the prehistoric gods who dispensed beverages to his people. The ancients drank the beverages during their ceremonial orgies and flew in the clouds with the god. That is said to be the meaning of the term *high*. I found it most interesting, as legend." Paoli looked at Owen with an anthropological interest, seeing him as a genuine prehistoric practitioner.

"We sure did, honey—with or without the orgies. And so did that crazy dame who made me last night—but where did *she* get the stuff?"

Paoli revealed her frustration. "I don't know that. I have not been able to locate your fabricator."

"Do me a big favor—don't ever find her."

"But she is responsible for you, for your present condition. I am certain that her unfortunate experiments with the beverage were responsible for your flawed construction and erratic behavior. That has never happened before. There has never been a faulty construct, before you, and it simply cannot be permitted to endure."

"Meaning what?"

"I must correct the error. You will have to be reconstructed in the proper manner."

He pointed. "Back into that oven?"

"Yes."

"Supposing I object? Supposing I take the Fourth Amendment?"

"It is my duty to the city."

Owen said, "I'm a variant, and a damned good one."

"You are a flawed variant. The flaw must be erased."

Owen prepared to run. He didn't know if he could outrun the long-legged blonde, but the doorway was open and he was always willing to try.

He asked, "So what do we do now? Fly kites?"

Paoli folded her arms and inspected him carefully, letting her gaze travel from head to toe and back again. Owen recognized the look in her eye; it was the same shown by Kehli as she sat on the blanket in the woods.

She said, "I admit to a certain curiosity."

"About what?"

"About you. About variables and their performances. I have wondered if your flaw was deliberately introduced to enhance the results."

Owen studied the traffic warden. A lively rubber ball of exhilaration snapped up and down his spine. "Do you want to find out?"

"In what way?"

"I'll cooperate with you, if you'll cooperate with me."

"Cooperate in what way?"

"Join me in the wake. That's an old prehistoric practice, just chock full of significance. We do it to keep the gods happy." Owen put his fingers on her chest and traced an imaginary T-square. "I'll show you all the secret rites of the good ol' Indiana boys, but you have to promise to keep the secrets. And after that you can pry and poke all you want—you can look for flaws and things —whatever makes you happy."

She looked down at his fingers. "What is expected of me?"

Owen placed the 1915 dime in her hand. "Hold that. Wrap it up in your fist and hold it tight. That's the year I was born."

Paoli obediently clutched the dime in a fist.

He held the 1943 dime in his left fist and picked up a bottle. "I'm holding the dead year, and now we're in tune with the ages. Down the hatch, baby doll."

"Down what hatch?"

"Never mind, just follow me. The redcoats are coming!"

Paoli watched him drink long and swallow easily.

Owen said, "*Ah . . .* now that's the way us old prehistoric guys do it." He gave up the bottle.

Paoli said dutifully, "The redcoats are coming." She did as Owen had done, swallowed, gasped for breath, and turned red in the face, crying, "*Oh . . . !*"

"Now this is going to be one damned fine wake," Owen declared, and whacked Paoli on the back to help her catch her breath. "It ain't everybody who can celebrate their own wake—not standing up, that is."

Seven

There are two times when you can never tell what is going to happen. One is when a man takes his first drink; the other is when a woman takes her latest.

— O. Henry

The first bottle lay on its back on the workbench, empty. The seal had been broken on the second bottle and the contents proved to be of a quality equal to the first. Owen Hall realized that he had missed his calling.

Paoli said, "I have asked you three times but you have not explained. Why is a wake?" She sprawled on a chair in the small space that served as a lounge area.

Owen was sitting on the floor not far from her feet, attempting to light a cigar. The match would not flame.

"What? When did you ask me three times?"

"You do not losten to me."

"I always listen to a lady when I can understand her. Your words are a little bit slurred."

"You did not explain a clothesline."

"I think I've missed a boat somewhere," Owen said. "One of us is going up like a kite."

"I asked you the *first* time when you were inspecting the chamber you call an oven. It is not an oven. You had your head inside the chamber—you said that it was too small and you would not fit." She regarded him owlishly, making a determined effort to control her speech. "You will fit."

Skeptically: "I'm of two minds about that. Now, what's this jazz about a clothesline?"

"I asked you the *second* time when you were in the shewer . . . uh, shower, washing with your clothes on. You replied that you were washing away the soot. There is no soot in the chamber."

He studied the match in his hand. "Son of a gun! That's why it won't light—it's wet."

Paoli hesitated, ran her tongue over her lips to assist in pronunciation, and said, "I asked you the *third* time while you were putting your clothing to dry in the sun. You complained that I had no clothesline."

"Oh *that* clothesline." Owen Hall snapped his fingers at the reminder. "They should be dry by now, I guess— it's been a while."

He struggled to his feet and ambled around the room divider to the doorway, facing the familiar heat of August. Owen stepped out into the bright afternoon sunshine and felt the heat on his bare body. His coveralls were laid out on the patch of grass just behind the doorway, baking in the sun. He knelt beside them and ran his fingers down inside a pocket to retrieve the remaining matches. The topside of the garment seemed done. He turned the coveralls over to let the backside have its time in the sun and then smoothed the arms and legs to dry without wrinkles. It paid to be neat. That done, Owen stood up to again scan the lush countryside and the rolling road.

The workmen riding past the house ignored him and his nudity. Clods. *He* wouldn't have ignored a naked man loafing on somebody's sidewalk if he had been in their place; *he* would have at least turned to stare and compare as he sped by. Owen looked over the heads of the uncurious zombies to the timber standing against the horizon, wanting to make sure it was still there, still solid and real and inviting. He caught a flash of pink against the trees.

Two rangy women were coming into town on the trot, following the beaten path between the cemetery and the roadway. Their manner suggested an urgency. It was easy to guess the snooping wardens had discovered his back trail.

It seemed prudent to go inside.

The tall blonde seemed in imminent danger of falling off her chair. She was listing to starboard and studying the floor with bemusement. Owen assisted her to a more stable position and sat down at her feet.

"Never mind the clothesline, baby doll—the greensward yonder is doing the job." He reached for the nearby bottle. "The redcoats are coming."

"Again?"

"Yep." Owen led the ritual.

Paoli obediently followed his lead. She swallowed hard and whispered, "That is a most potent beverage."

"That is also the last bottle. I've got my work cut out for me, honeypot. The redcoats are closing in."

She looked down at him carefully and her eyes widened. "You do not have your clothes on."

"What a keen eye you have!" Owen cried. "Somebody forgot to make the underwear. I wear a size thirty-two, if you feel like whipping up a batch."

She pointed a finger. "The fourth time you have not answered the question."

"What question?"

"Why is a wake?"

Owen considered that and scratched the hair on his chest. "Well, I don't know why. It just *is*, that's all. It's a grand old tradition like Mom, apple pie, and flags."

"What does a wake do?"

"Honey, we're doing it. The guest of honor doesn't have to do anything, of course—he doesn't even have to make a speech. Now usually, the neighbors all come in and pay their respects and tell a lot of lies about the dear departed. That's all part of the ritual, you understand —lying about how good and noble and true the fella was. I guess it keeps the elder gods happy." Owen blew on a match head to make certain it was dry and finally succeeded in lighting the cigar. "The folks sit around eating and drinking and lying a lot, and come sunrise everybody goes home well satisfied with themselves. They've done their duty. Somebody keeps the widow company so she won't grieve all night. If she happens to be a doll, you can bet some guy will stay the night with her. And that's a wake."

Paoli stared at the cigar with fascination. "It is a strange ritual with strange symbols. Will you stay the night?"

"You couldn't drive me away with an elephant."

"I don't have an elefent . . . elephant. Is that like a clothesline?"

"Not on Tuesday," Owen replied. He waved the cigar toward the open doorway. "This town ain't got no park benches, and the hounds of the law are yapping at my heels. You bet I'm going to stay the night—it's my wake. Kelly is to blame—Kelly and that old bat. Between the two of *them* they put me in this fix, so you've got to do the right thing by me."

"I have said that I would."

He looked up at the woman teetering on the chair, sizing her. "I wish you were shorter."

"Why?"

"You're too tall for me. I wish you were my size."

"I will adjust."

The woman very slowly and carefully slipped off the chair and knelt on the floor beside Owen, looking down on him from a height. Owen shook his head. It was still necessary to crane his neck to look up and inspect that delightful freckle on the tip of her nose.

"Not enough adjustment."

Paoli teetered, nearly lost her balance, and abruptly sat down beside him. The impact was jarring.

He was quickly solicitous. "How's your equilibrium?"

"A shoe."

"You don't have shoes on. You took them off when you came into the shower to haul me out."

"Askew."

He sat up straight beside her to measure his body against hers and found himself at shoulder level. "You're still a head taller," was the complaint.

Paoli stretched out on the floor by toppling backward, coming down much harder than intended. The floor shook.

"Mother!"

"I usually say *fudge*," Owen commented. He measured the long pink length by eyeball and then lay down beside her, snuggling up against the wet coveralls to obtain the more accurate measurement. His eye level was at her chest.

"Nope," he said after a lengthy study. "Too long."

"I can do no more!" Paoli cried. "Your gods are hard to appease."

"I'm not worried about the gods right now—I'm thinking of me. Let me figure on it."

Paoli struggled to sit up. She made it on the second try but had to brace her hands on the floor to maintain the position. The floor seemed strangely unsteady.

"I am naturally taller than you—females are always taller than males. My mother was tall."

"Did your father stand on a chair?"

"I had no father."

Owen squinted up at the woman and wondered if she had reached her capacity. That was the trouble with newcomers—they usually had to stop drinking long before the party was over. He sat up beside her and patted her shoulder.

"Everybody has a father," he explained patiently. "I guess you never got the birds-and-bees lecture; I guess they don't tell you the facts of life around here. No father, no child—us men are necessary for that. And judging by the number of women I've seen in this here town, there must be a *busy* bunch of variants hanging around."

"Males are *not* necessary," she contradicted. "Males are used only for labor in the city. The Mother practices parthenogenesis to maintain a planned female population."

"Nope, never heard of that religion," Owen admitted. "Is it like the Baptists or more like the Unitarians?"

"It isn't a religion, it is the scientific method of causing pregnancy. Parthenogenesis is the reproduction of female children without the necessity of a male parent."

"You mean two women?" Owen fell back in astonishment. "Two women can *do it?*"

"Two or more."

"It won't work!" he declared. "That kind of funny business won't work. You've got to have a man."

"Our long history is proof enough. The city has been maintained for a hundred and sixty-nine years."

"Yeah—by *man*power."

"Females are responsible for the manpower. Females reproduce themselves."

Owen was so shaken that he reached for the bottled fortifier. "I'll be kicked by a cross-eyed mule!" He gaped up at his hostess. "*You* were born because of . . . uh . . . well, *two women* . . . doing things?"

"Myself, and the others."

"Geez, and here I thought I knew everything. I'm a man of the world." He stared at Paoli with continuing amazement. "Baby doll, they don't even do *that* in Indianapolis!"

"We must maintain our population."

Owen shook his head with dismay. "Just wait until Pastor Coulson gets here and finds out about *that*."

He swallowed and absently passed over the bottle.

Paoli said, "The redcoats are coming."

"Fat lot of good it'll do them in this town," Owen mumbled.

He got the warden on her feet after a long effort.

Moving carefully, lest she tumble to the floor and cause him to lose another several minutes getting her upright again, Owen led Paoli across the workshop to the machine. Her feet had some difficulty in following one another in a reasonably straight line. The coffin resting beside the oven door was pushed aside, and the door yanked open.

It was going to be a tight fit. The woman was much too long for the opening.

"What are we doing?" Paoli asked.

"We are conducting a scientific experiment, baby doll. We are going to whittle you down to size. I just figured out how to do it—all I have to do is trim a few inches off your legs and *presto!* bring you down eyeball to eyeball. I'm going to pop you into the oven and make shorter legs."

"Insert me into that chamber?"

"It's the only game in the house."

"But you aren't familiar with the machine."

"I am too! I made bacon all day."

"You don't know how to refashion a human body."

Owen stopped short, realizing the truth of the statement. Making bacon and booze and cigars was one thing, but making a woman—He glanced over at the instruction manuals on the workbench, but the memory of those livid man pictures reacted all the way down to his sphincter.

"Well, hey— Can't you tell me how to do it?"

"I suppose so. Yes. I know how."

"Now that's the answer! You tell me what to do and I'll press the buttons. See how simple it is?"

Simple.

Owen began the task of inserting the tall woman into the chamber, into his new operating theater. It was most difficult, even with her fumbling cooperation. On the first attempt he managed to stuff into the oven her head, shoulders, torso, and pelvis, but that left her legs and feet dangling outside over the oven door. The legs couldn't be shortened while they were outside the chamber and kicking. Owen hauled the body out, turned it around, and slid it in a second time. Paoli was bent nearly double. The posterior went in first, followed by torso, shoulders, and head. The arms were mostly inside, but her knees were hooked over the edge and the feet were still on the floor. Owen tried sliding her in on her back, and then on her belly. He bent the body double once again and inserted the head and feet together, but that left her rump hanging over into the room. Paoli tried to be helpful, but her rubbery limbs had a tendency to stray in the wrong directions.

Owen hauled the nonfitting body out of the operating theater and uttered an ancient, expressive Indiana word.

"Think!" he urged the woman.

"I am unable to think. My head spins."

"You need a stiff drink—it's good for fevers, dizzy spells, and frostbite. And you're dirty." Her wet clothes had picked up the soot or dust or whatever it was from inside the chamber. "You need a stiff drink and a bath. Do you a world of good."

Paoli said, "A wake is not amusing. I would not care to live in prehistoric times."

"Just between you and me, toots, I don't think much of *this* time—your time. I had more fun in Indiana—old nineteen forty-two was a good year, war or no war. Did I ever tell you about Shut Out?"

"What is a shutout?"

"A horse, a winner named Shut Out."

"What is a horse?"

Owen clicked his tongue. "Maybe you didn't get very far in school. Shut Out was one hell of a racehorse, if I say so myself, and, baby, I'm a keen judge of horse-flesh. Shut Out won the Derby last year and I made a bundle."

Paoli opened her mouth to ask but Owen held up a quick hand to stop the question.

"A bundle is ninety dollars. Now let's figure on this business at hand. We've got to whittle you down."

Owen studied the chamber's dimensions and then those of the blonde; he was already familiar with most of hers, but he enjoyed studying them nevertheless. Had she been his own height the problem wouldn't be a problem: the oven was designed for bodies six feet or shorter, and pity the poor basketball player if Kehli and her crew dug up a lanky male. At just six feet, his head would be touching one end of the chamber with his bare feet scraping the other end—with no thought for his comfort while the fabricator fiddled—but the leggy woman couldn't possibly fit inside unless she had the skills of a contortionist and the patience of a clutch of saints.

"I could put you up on the workbench and make the alterations first," Owen suggested. "I could whittle out a few inches here and there between knee and shinbone, and *then* pop you into the oven and glue you together again. I'm a pretty good master joiner, if I say so myself."

Paoli hugged her knees. "No."

"I didn't think you'd like that one—queasy stomach, I guess. Well, what to do, what to do?" He looked around the apartment. "Hey—I've got it! Stay right there now —don't go away."

She revealed no desire to get up from the floor.

Owen ran to the lounge area and came back with the chair Paoli had been sitting on earlier—a rather stiff and uncomfortable straight chair without arms or seat padding.

"I saw Abbott and Costello do this with a horse—except that they were trying to get up on top, of course."

"Shut Out," she said.

"Exactly. You're coming along, baby doll."

Owen directed his subject to crawl inside the chamber feet first, scrunching in all the way until her toes touched the farthest corner—but remembering to keep her legs straight, of course. Paoli went in slowly: feet, legs, pelvis, and most of the torso. Owen pulled the chair up to the oven door and positioned it under her shoulders and head. For the first time he had all of her off the floor, with the entire body in a horizontal position.

"Eureka!" he cried with satisfaction. "That's using the old noggin. Are you comfy, honeypot?"

"No."

"Pay it no mind. This won't take long."

Owen ran around to the front of the machine and met the next obstacle: the concave bar and the viewing window were much too high for his forehead and eyes, being designed for tall operation. He considered getting another chair but realized that would put him too high in the air. The apartment had no footstools or buckets to stand on. Owen peered around the corner at Paoli, and then beyond her to rediscover Yorick's mummy case.

He pulled the coffin into position at the front of the machine and gingerly stood on it to test its strength. The lid supported his weight. Owen's forehead touched the cerebral bar.

"Facile Lucille, I've got it!" He peered into the dim chamber and saw the pink-clad legs stretched out before him, awaiting the journeyman carpenter's magic touch. The only light in the operating theater was the daylight filtering through the front doorway.

"I'm ready, loveboat—it won't be long now. That's a joke, if you missed it. What do I do first?"

"Depress the first button."

"Just like making bacon." Owen pushed but nothing happened. He jabbed the button a second time. "Something wrong here. Is the power off?"

"It is never off. Depress the button firmly."

Owen pushed in and held it down with his thumb. "I did, I *did,* but there ain't nothing happening. There's no work light, no paper tray, no nothing. What's the matter?"

"Depress the second button."

Owen pressed without result and then methodically pushed all the buttons in sequence. The machine did nothing. He pushed in reverse sequence. There was no result.

"This tool of the devil won't work! It's extinct, defunct, cold stone dead. You forgot to pay the electric bill—the power is off."

"It isn't working for you?"

"It isn't working for me and you. Dead as the old doornail." He balled a fist and beat on the machine.

After a thoughtful silence Paoli said, "I see."

"I don't see much of anything. Just you in there."

"The machine cannot operate while the door is open. This door I am lying on. It is a safety measure."

Owen blinked at the dim legs seen behind the window and then sat down on the coffin to contemplate his defeat. He gazed about the apartment, taking a mental inventory of the cramped lounge, the woman's bedroom, the dining area, the kitchen, that cubicle at the back where he was supposed to sleep, and finally the workshop. He looked without real interest at the jar of old coins on the bench. The pile of kindling wood from the broken door was heaped at the front of the parlor—if he wanted to stretch a point and call the entranceway a parlor. The road continued to move under the bright sun. None of it really mattered. He had lost a battle to the machine— his first loss of the day. The sense of failure depressed him.

The woman slowly hauled herself out of the oven, tumbled off the chair, picked herself up, and came around the corner to sit on the coffin beside him.

The lid sank under their weight.

She said in explanation, "The circuitry includes a safety switch at the door; it is there to prevent a mishap during the reconstitution processes. I didn't remember that because my head spins."

"Never mind, just never mind." Owen reached for her hand and gently squeezed her fingers in reassurance. "I *like* tall women."

They sat together for a long while in contemplative silence, holding hands and watching a small part of the world pass by the doorway. Workmen continued to go by in their familiar wooden poses, and once a pink-clad monitor turned to stare in wonder at the doorless doorway, but she didn't leave the road to investigate the oddity. Owen had forgotten his clothing lying out on the grass.

He wondered if that door and its switch was the clue to his second lifestyle. Had the drunken bat of last night opened the oven door too soon and hauled him out halfbaked, in a manner of speaking? Had she failed to follow the timing of the recipe, being too eager to get her hands on his body? *If* she was hot for his body. Or had she simply been so loaded on bad booze that she didn't know what she was doing and couldn't read the instruction book?

Paoli was looking at his hand enfolding hers. "Do you have a name?"

"Of course I have a name. I've already told you my name. My name is Owen Hall. I'm from Indiana."

"You seem sad, Owen Hall from Indiana."

"That's because I can't be a zeppelin pilot," he said. "I always wanted to be a zeppelin pilot, but now I can't be because it crashed in Jersey about six years ago and I don't think they make them anymore, what with the war and all."

The woman shook her head with puzzlement and then wished that she hadn't. "I don't understand you *again*, Owen Hall from Indiana."

"I thought you'd ask, what is a zeppelin?"

"What is a zeppelin?"

"Baby doll, I just happen to be a zeppelin expert. As a matter of cold fact, I'm the only guy in this here town that knows anything about anything. I wonder if I could get a job as mayor, or prince, or something like that, and put my talents to work?" Owen rested the whiskey bottle on his knee and debated the wisdom of offering the woman a drink. She was having some difficulty in maintaining her perch on the coffin. "A zeppelin is a big gas bag that sails around in the sky. People ride in it—they ride in those little cars slung underneath the bag."

"Did the ancient gods walk on the sky with it?"

"They sure did. Most of the time they rode in airplanes, but some of the rich ones had zeppelins. I saw one once—a real one."

Paoli said in awe, "You are a living legend."

Owen eyed her suspiciously, searching for mockery.

"I was about fourteen years old when a real monster of a zeppelin sailed right over my head—sailed right across Indiana. Wow, but it was big! That old gas bag was over seven hundred feet long and I'll bet you it was a hundred feet in diameter—it was huge! I remember that it had five engines—I counted them—and the next day the papers said it was zipping along at seventy miles an hour. Lovepot, that's speed.

"It was on a round-the-world tour. It flew over Siberia and Japan and Alaska. Well, it actually flew all the way around the world, and then it flew over Indiana on the way home. *That's* when I decided that I wanted to be a zeppelin pilot and fly around the world—or fly over the

North Pole like that Italian zeppelin did in nineteen twenty-six." He held the bottle up to his eye, measuring the remaining contents. "But now I can't. There ain't no more zeppelins—ol' Hitler had them broken up for scrap —and here I sit stuck away in this crazy place with a lady who's so loaded she's about to fall right off this here coffin. There ain't no justice."

."The old Mother stories are *true*," Paoli exclaimed. "Gods *did* walk the sky in ancient times."

"We called them fly-boys."

"Are you an ancient fly-boy?"

"Nope, I'm an ancient Democrat—vote early and often."

Owen took a final drink from his bottle, firmly capped it, and set it aside. There was work to do, and he began the difficult task of getting the woman to her feet and into the shower stall. She didn't cooperate readily because she didn't understand what was happening.

"Is the wake ended?"

"The wake is *not* ended. I came over to stay the night, remember?" He tried to brush away the sooty debris but succeeded only in smearing the pink coveralls. "We've got to get you cleaned up. You look a mess."

"I have now cloothing."

"New clothing."

"I have new clothing."

"Your face and hands are dirty, and some of the oven stuff is in your hair. You need a bath."

Owen grasped her forearms and began tugging. Paoli did nothing but sit and stare at him. Her eyes would not focus properly. Owen tried to encircle her waist with his arms and lift her off the coffin, but failed because he lacked the proper purchase to move her mass. He thought that perhaps a goose in the proper place would start her skyward, but it did not—she merely looked around and down at him in startled surprise. Finally, Owen rapped sharply on the side of the coffin with his knuckles.

She asked with wonder, "Who is that?" and looked at the doorless doorway.

Owen said, "Poor Yorick wants out of the coffin. You're sitting on his stomach."

Paoli jumped and would have toppled over face for-

ward onto the floor if Owen had not steadied her. He led
her into the shower stall.

It was a small cubicle, barely large enough for the
two of them, but he managed to crowd in with her and
turn on the water. She gasped when the cold stream
struck her on top of the head and coursed down her
face.

Owen said sheepishly, "I forgot to take your clothes
off." He found the fasteners and peeled off the soggy
coveralls. Paoli watched him wordlessly.

"No fair!" Owen cried, and pointed to the halter serving as a bra. "You make underwear for yourself, but
nobody made any for me." He reached around behind
her and unfastened the halter, then slipped his fingers
into the waistline of the underpants and pulled them
down and off. When he straightened up he found his
eye level just above the nipples of her breasts.

Owen held his silence for a long moment and finally
expelled a breath. "Geez, babe. I don't know what to
say."

Paoli continued to watch him without speaking.

After a while Owen remembered his manners. "Got
any soap?"

She gave him a small bar of soap. Owen made suds
and began soaping her down, beginning with her neck
and working down her arms. By the time he had reached
her hands and the tips of her fingers he had regained a
measure of courage. The amazon's breasts no longer
intimidated him. Owen lifted her hands up to his shoulders and began soaping her torso. He lingered over the
breasts long after they were impeccably clean, and
moved down to wash her stomach. After a very long
time he found himself at her knees.

"Hey, move your feet apart. You're too tight."

Paoli complied.

When the task was half completed Owen turned the
woman around and washed up the back, beginning at
the heels and working toward the neck. He was back at
the beginning. There was no shampoo to be found in the
cubicle, so he washed her hair with soap and then rinsed
it two or three times to be certain the soap was gone. The
task was done and he turned off the water. The woman
leaned against the stall with her eyes closed.

"Don't go to sleep, toots. You can't sleep here."

She answered quietly, "I am not sleeping, Owen Hall."

He led her from the stall and looked around for a towel. There was one, for the two of them.

Owen said, "Come along. We'll dry outside." He picked up the towel and took her hand. They left two trails of water across the floor from the shower to the front door. Owen thought the hot sun felt extraordinarily fine on his bare skin after the cascade of cold water.

The traveling zombies ignored them.

Owen positioned Paoli in the center of the small lawn with her body facing the western sun and asked her to bend toward him. When she did he began toweling her hair. Owen rubbed briskly, looking over her head at the men on the road. It occurred to him that this was the acid test: if just one of them turned to stare, or even peeked through slitted fingers, at the two naked bodies on the grass, *that* man was more alive than dead. None of them exhibited the spark of life, either above or below.

When the woman's hair was dry to his satisfaction, he stood her straight and rubbed down the tall, lithe body. The sun had already done most of the work for him, but he considered it his duty to towel the entire body nonetheless. She might catch mildew if moisture remained anywhere on the long frame. Owen enjoyed his work. He threw himself into the job with enthusiasm, toweling down and up and around and down again, even remembering to lift each foot and dry the bottom of it. When he patted her knees in signal, she spread her feet apart without the necessity of words. All in all, Owen spent ten or fifteen minutes at the happy task, and when he stopped because his arms were getting tired, he flipped the towel over his shoulder and stepped back to inspect Paoli.

Two pink-clad monitors were standing on the grass at the edge of the road, inspecting them. Their mouths hung open with astonishment.

There had been no warning of their arrival.

"Good afternoon, ladies." Owen thought it best to placate them—he didn't want to lose his prize now. "You're looking tired and careworn. Are you in the mood for a bath and a brisk rub? I have the expert's touch." He demonstrated the expert's touch by playing the tips of his fingers up and down Paoli's spine. She shivered, but not from a chill.

The monitors could only gape at him, now amazed by a talking male. One of them began the automatic motion of reaching out, reaching for his breast pocket to check his identification, but her hand quickly dropped away when she remembered that the talking male was unclothed. Her gaze went down his body and lingered on his thighs.

Owen took the blonde's hand and led her inside. He paused in the doorway to glance back at the staring monitors and found that they had not yet recovered their wits. One stared at his backside.

"Cleanliness is next to godliness," Owen said, and disappeared into the dim recesses of the house.

Paoli lay on her bed looking up at Owen. She was unblinking, unmoving, and content to merely watch him.

"Want to dance now, baby doll?"

She asked, "Will we dance all night?"

Owen began a grin but changed it to a soft smile and sat down beside her on the bed. His weight caused her to roll toward him. He studied her face for a moment and then, despite himself, let his gaze drift down the long silken body. Paoli was pink.

"We'll dance until you holler quit," he promised.

"Did the ancients do this at the wakes?"

"They did, unless the guest of honor objected. He usually didn't say much."

Paoli waited, looking up at him.

Owen patted her knees in the now familiar signal and Paoli responded.

Eight

A woman is a foreign land,
Of which, though there he settle young,
A man will ne'er quite understand
The customs, politics and tongue.
                              —Coventry Patmore

Owen Hall opened his eyes and saw the ceiling. It wasn't a readily familiar ceiling—it was nothing he remembered from any old room in Indiana—and he stared at it for a long moment of disorientation. The ceiling was washed in fading daylight, and the room was hot. Owen rolled his head on the bed to look across the room, but an opaque divider blocked his view. That was familiar. The daylight was coming from some point on the other side of the divider, but the source eluded him. He listened carefully for people sounds, traffic sounds, but there were none—and then, suddenly, he remembered where he was and why the sunlight was spilling across the ceiling.

"Oh, my." His mouth was as dry as popcorn.

Owen turned his head the other way on the bed and discovered he was only inches away from the sleeping woman. She was on her side facing away from him, with one leg flung carelessly toward his side of the bed. He glanced down at the leg and then followed it upward to the body.

"Oh, my!" he said again.

He couldn't guess how long he'd been sleeping, but

the setting sun offered a clue. All the rest of it was crystal clear—he remembered the shower and the rubdown in the sun, the gawking women outside, and then going to bed with Paoli; he remembered what they had done and the length of time they'd taken while doing it; he remembered her amazement at learning a new thing and his amazement at discovering that she wasn't a virgin, but he couldn't guess or judge how long he'd slept afterward. And now he was hungry. Dry in the mouth and hungry. Dancing certainly took a lot out of a man.

Owen slipped out of bed and padded around the room divider to look through the gaping doorway.

The August sun was low in the west and casting long shadows of men on the road. He approached the doorway, but caution prompted him to stop just inside the battered frame, just out of sight of those on the roadway. The hounds of the law were still searching for him.

"Confound it, they just won't give up."

The road was teeming with hundreds of homebound workmen, all of them stolidly facing the east and riding that long circle around the city to their destinations. The road was also populated with an unusual number of female monitors inspecting the zombies—testing them, thumping them, attempting to provoke them into a response, picking at their identification bars. The continued search meant that they had not yet turned up the gravedigger who was now wearing Owen's number. He suspected that the town police force had called out the reserves; their number was double and perhaps triple the number he'd seen on the road early in the morning.

Owen stayed out of sight, knowing it prudent to not retrieve his clothing just then. The dry coveralls were stretched out on the grass where he'd left them and it was his good fortune that none of the monitors saw them or bothered to come inspect them and then peer into the empty doorway.

The doggers were eager to find him, but they were plainly amateurs at this manhunting business; they lacked the technique. If *he* were the mayor or the marshall of the town, he could teach *them* a thing or two. That's what this town needed—organization all the way down the line.

The monitors weren't skilled huntresses, they didn't have the good old American know-how of the Indiana

cops, or else they would have organized a door-to-door
search long before now. The missing door to *this* house
should have alerted them, should have tipped them that
something unusual was happening inside, if nothing more
than a burglary, but instead of investigating the doorless
place they wasted their time by poking men on the road.
Owen shook his head at the inept search.

They actually expected him to play dumb; they really
thought he was so dumb that he'd be out there skylark-
ing on the road all the while they were searching for him.
It didn't speak for efficient police work, but it did say
that his kind was very rare—so rare that the monitors
lacked a businesslike system of finding him. It was silly
that the pair of gaping women who had discovered him
naked on the grass earlier in the afternoon never realized he was the culprit they sought. Silly and dumb. An
Indiana cop would have nailed his tail to the wall in
seconds, and the explanations would have come later.

Kehli and Paoli had been literally truthful when they
had said that a man like him had never happened in the
city before. Variants were made now and then for the
amusement and edification of some woman, and perhaps
once in a while a bad rebuilding job rolled out of the
oven, but *he* seemed to be the one and only bungled variant in the town's history. One hundred and sixty-nine
years of female history, unless these people had short
memories.

Owen backed away from the door and returned to the
workbench in search of the cigars and a drink. His
mouth was still dry and he wished mightily for a long
cold beer, but the bourbon would have to do. It was still
mellow but warm. The pile of old coins spilled on the
bench took his attention and he pushed them about with
a finger, arranging the dates in a rough consecutive order.

The hole in history bothered him.

These people—the women and the zombies—had
lived in the city for 169 years (they said), but before
them there was something else called the NorAmerFed,
and before *that* there was the good old U.S. of A. Well,
maybe, just maybe. History things didn't always follow
along in a neat, orderly manner. Old nations didn't just
stop at sundown one day and let a new nation spring up
at sunrise the next morning—it wasn't as easy as all that,

as one of his Indiana schoolteachers had pounded into his head. There was usually something in between the end of one government and the beginning of the next, and that something in between was likely to be a bloody mess, a disaster, even a revolution. There was likely to be a nothing space of months or years to pass the time while people got things organized and running smoothly again.

Take the dates on these coins, for instance.

Here was a half-dollar dated 1984, so the United States was still chugging along in 1984, no matter who won the war and no matter if the picture of *that* jackass was stamped on the coin. Owen examined it closely. There were no foreign words on the coin—nothing printed in German, Italian, or Japanese—which certainly suggested that the Americans had won the war after all. Comforting notion. But how long did the United States last *after* 1984? No clue. And when the country finally stopped being the United States and fell down, how long was the something in between until people got this NorAmerFed business organized and running well? No clue.

The new Feds minted ten shul pieces in 2081 and 2097, and *that* was . . . *that* was only ninety-seven to a 113 years after 1984. Not very long—not long at all. And yet there was still Paoli's history to be accounted for —another 169 years to be added to all the other figures. He counted on his fingers, made an obvious error, and went back to count again. All of it—everything and the kitchen sink—made *this* year out to be 2266. August 2266 A.D. Imagine it: that long! And 2266 take away 1943, when life had stopped for him the first time, was . . . was at least 323 years! All that without even counting the blank spaces in between governments—the nothing spaces before each new country was organized and working. Why, if he made proper allowances for the blanks between nations, if he allowed for a blank between the United States and the NorAmerFed, and yet another blank between the NorAmerFed and the Queen Bee's cities, it was possible that five hundred or a thousand years had passed since that wintry night in 1943 when he died at a railroad crossing. A thousand years.

It boggled the mind.

Owen found it difficult to believe that he'd been below

ground for five hundred or a thousand years waiting for Kehli to dig him up only yesterday. Why, that was fantastic. What's more, he'd *rot*.

He had a drink on it, contemplating rotting.

Well, no—maybe not. Maybe his bones wouldn't rot after all. He was every bit as good as a king or a slave, and the scientists were always digging up kings and slaves and other people who had lived two or three thousand years ago over there in Palestine and Turkey and Egypt and foreign places like that. They were finding kings all the time; buried kings were knocking around all over Egypt. The scientists dug up the bones and the mummies and put them in museums, and then the *Tribune* reporters wrote articles about them. Owen had read all about the latest scientific discoveries in the Chicago *Tribune;* he prided himself on his scholarship and often wondered if he'd missed his calling.

The Sunday magazine sections were vast storehouses of wisdom and knowledge.

About ten years ago—no, come to think on it, it happened in 1930—thirteen years ago another scientist named Tombaugh had been puttering around in his observatory and found a brand-new planet named Pluto, away out to hell and gone beyond Saturn. It was a tiny planet—an icy thing. The magazine section of the *Tribune* had printed a lengthy piece on the discovery together with pictures of Mr. Tombaugh, his telescope, his blinker machine, and drawings of what the surface of Pluto looked like: it was all frozen seas, with huge rocks and mountaintops sticking up through the ice. Owen remembered comparing the pictures of Pluto to the mountains and ice fields of the South Pole.

On another Sunday about four years ago, just before the war started in Europe, there had been a fine article on a scientist named Munnfred and a three-thousand-year-old tomb he'd uncovered in Mesopotamia, which was in one of those foreign places like Iran or Iraq.

The newspaper had printed photographs and sketches of the tomb. Dr. Munnfred said the bones in a royal chamber were fully three thousand years old, and the artifacts in the chamber identified the remains as that of a woman, one of the concubines of King Gilgamesh. The newspaper artist offered a picture of Gilgamesh, based on ancient but authentic records. The king wore his hair down to his waist and looked like a red radical bolshevik.

Owen realized the significance of that discovery now. It made *him* authentic.

If the concubine's bones could endure for three thousand years and then be found and identified by Dr. Munnfred, it was likely that *his* bones could last for five hundred or a thousand years and be found by Kehli and her crew. The only difference being that Kehli was a grave robber, not a trained scientist, but Owen decided he could forgive her that. It was pretty nice being alive again a thousand years in the future, even if the town *was* a rum place to be alive in.

Owen played with the coins, turning the matter over in his mind. Imagine it! Perhaps he *was* a thousand years old—a bungled variant who was the oldest man on earth. Paster Coulson would be mighty surprised when the grave robbers turned *him* up.

He needed clean clothing.

Owen prowled about the blonde's bedroom inspecting the merchandise available to him. The blonde was sprawled on the rumpled bed, sleeping like an exhausted rug cutter, but he knew better than to wake her. Moving quietly, Owen picked among the underclothing.

There were several pairs of short white socks that felt like cotton. He tried on a pair and found that they fitted him to just above the ankles. Underpants were another matter. The blonde owned several pair of white cottony underpants, but Owen wasn't at all sure he wanted to be caught dead in them. The underpants were a trifle longer than the boxer shorts he was used to, but not quite as long as the bloomers his grandmother had worn in her heyday. Strange that he hadn't noticed the cut and style of those underpants when he pulled a pair off the blonde in the shower. Perhaps his mind had been on other things —perhaps he'd been distracted by one thing or another. Owen decided he didn't want to wear the underpants.

The pink coveralls were a sloppy fit, of course, but they were better than the drab ones he'd been wearing. He climbed into the coveralls and rolled up the sleeves and legs to accommodate his shorter frame. All in all, not too bad for hand-me-down clothing. Even the blonde's shoes were a decent fit.

The back door claimed his attention. He hadn't yet inspected the outback, but it might provide a handy escape route. Road travel was becoming risky to him.

The house—or the apartment—narrowed at the back, with the rear wall of the trapezoid being only wide enough to accommodate the door and the back wall of the small bedroom where zombies were expected to sleep on a cot. The back door was fastened with a simple sliding bolt and Owen found time to wonder why. There seemed to be no such thing as crime in the city, so why bother to bolt a door? He opened it and another kind of jungle met his eye.

The outback was an overgrown confusion of weeds and pipes in contrasting array. The weeds were a tangled jungle, having never known a scythe or a lawn mower, while the pipes had been put down in neat patterns resembling the spokes of a wheel. There were no fences or walks, no gardens or garden paths, not even a scrawny tree—nothing but weeds and conduits. Owen counted pipes of three sizes: small three-inch pipes that likely carried water to each dwelling, larger six-inch pipes that carried he knew not what, and even larger twenty-inch ducts that resembled heating ducts above coal furnaces —but these surely couldn't be heating pipes for the winter months for the heat losses would be enormous. The pipes were all aboveground, and a set of three served each house.

Owen dropped to the ground and put an ear to the smallest pipe. As expected, he heard water running. The next largest size gave him no hint of what it carried or contained; it was warm with the heat of the day but betrayed no sound to his ear. If this was good old Indiana, he'd guess it for a gas pipe of enormous size. The largest duct was as much a mystery as the supposed gas pipe. It too was warm from the sun, but there was no clue to its purpose. Paoli's house had neither heating nor air conditioning, as far as he could determine, and he'd cased it carefully. The lack of a heating system and the presence of water pipes aboveground told him the town enjoyed mild winters; he guessed they'd never seen snow and ice around here.

Owen tested the largest duct for strength and then climbed atop it to peer inward, toward the center of the circle city. A large building he thought of as the powerhouse was there, in the geographical center, and all the pipes radiated from it. Each house was served by three pipes, and each set of three ran toward the powerhouse; the sets of three converged before they reached the powerhouse to larger, fewer pipes and then vanished into the building. The plan was an enormous wheel with the powerhouse serving as the hub and hundreds—perhaps even a thousand—spokes stretching out to serve each dwelling.

"Well, I can't knock it," he said aloud. "It works, and Hartford City can't say as much all the time."

He jumped down from the duct and thought to test the doors to either side of Paoli's house. Both the doors were locked. Perhaps the occupants kept them locked to forestall the plumbers working in the backyard jungle; a lazy workman mending a water pipe just might wander through an unlocked door and take a nap on the cot inside.

Owen went inside but left his escape hatch unlocked.

The tired blonde was still sleeping flat on the bed with arms and legs akimbo. He looked at the long body for a fanciful moment but again decided against waking her and offering another smoochy session. His desire was there—the spirit and the flesh were most willing—but he knew from experience that sleeping partners didn't always appreciate a sudden arousal and a repeat performance. They were apt to be rude at such times.

Owen retraced his steps to the workbench, sampled the bourbon, decided against a cigar for the time being, and gathered up a couple of screwdrivers. It was time to replace the front door.

The better way would be to manufacture one in the think-and-do machine, a splendid door to display his skills as a master carpenter and one that would be the envy of all the neighbors in the morning, but he had already learned that the oven was much too small to build a door in one piece. The leggy blonde wouldn't fit into the oven for a simple restructuring job, therefore a new door to accommodate the height of the leggy blonde would be equally impossible. Of course, there *would* be large machines somewhere in the manufacturing district that were capable of producing doors, but he couldn't run down to the manufacturing district just now.

There were handy substitutes all about.

Owen peered through the opening, alert for a challenge from a suspicious monitor. There were none in the vicinity. A few scattered workmen still rode the rolling road but the great bulk of them had disappeared into the warrens along the way. In the far distance, to the northeast, three monitors were working the road but the moving belt was carrying them away from him. He stepped out onto the lawn, self-confident in his new pink uniform, and turned away from the monitors toward the southwest. The next-door neighbor had a nice lavender door.

Owen removed the screws from the hinges and dropped them into a pocket. When the door was free of its fastenings he eased it away from the frame to disengage the lock—if there *was* a lock on the opposite side —and pulled the panel free of the striker plate. The door was his. The interior of the neighboring house was dark, and he was pleased at the absence of an outcry. Owen carried it across the grass, fitted it into Paoli's doorframe, and came a cropper.

"Look at it!" he cried his disgust. "Just look at the double-damned thing! An apprentice could do better."

The borrowed door was half an inch too wide to fit into the frame. The height was right and the flapping hinges lined up with all but one of the screw holes, but the door would not close firmly until half an inch was trimmed off the latch side.

Owen yanked the misfitting door out of the frame and stalked out to the rolling road.

"Hey, you, Barney!" he yelled at a workman.

The zombie ignored him.

Owen hopped onto the road and chased after the man. The door was under his arm. When he caught up to the obstinate fellow he planted himself firmly in front of the dulled eyes and flashed pink. Owen put his free hand beneath the man's chin and raised his head to see the pink. The workman exhibited a minute spark of recognition. He stared at the pink coveralls, looked up at Owen's face, and dropped his gaze to the coveralls at chest height.

"Now you're getting the idea, Barney. Don't let my voice fool you—I'm a ventriloquist." He transferred the stolen door to the workman. The man almost dropped it. "Hold it!" Owen ordered. "Hold it tight."

The zombie clutched the door with both hands.

"Now you've got the idea, Barney. Listen closely—this is an order. Are you listening?"

The zombie made no answer.

"Good man," Owen said approvingly. "You know the score. I'm wearing pink and pink is the boss around here. Now then, hold on to this door and don't lose it. Take the door home with you. If *anybody* asks where you got it, tell them you won it in a poker game. Got all that?"

The worker held the door as if it were treasure.

Owen clapped him on the shoulder. "You're a fine fellow, Barney. If I see you in the bar I'll buy you a drink. Go along now."

He hopped off the road and watched while the zombie rode away to the northeast, carrying his new possession.

Owen trotted back to the two open doorways and cast about for another likely door. Paoli's neighbor on the opposite side had a pale yellow door, and Owen promptly went to work on the retaining screws.

The yellow door didn't fit; it was too small and allowed a large gap on the latch side. Owen expressed his opinion of the carpentry skills prevalent in the town and compared the misfitting doors to the poor meat he'd had on the picnic in the woods. The slave labor hereabouts may be cheap and compliant, but it wasn't worth a damn when it came down to quality workmanship; somebody just wasn't fitting the man to the job. The rejected yellow door was given to another traveler on the road with the same instructions.

Owen pulled five doors before he found a winner.

The fifth and last door was a wretched shade of green, but, what the hell, it fitted smoothly and Owen was satisfied. The door hung well, balanced nicely, all the screw holes had lined up, and the latch went into the striker plate without fault, so he pronounced it a success and went inside for a well-deserved drink. Two drinks. (He'd have to do something about refilling the bottle.) Paoli would be pleased with her nice new door when she woke up, and meanwhile, somewhere in the town, four proud workmen were carrying home their winnings.

He heard a whining moan in the bedroom.

Owen ambled around the room divider, carrying the bottle to lift the lady's spirits.

"Hello, there, tootsy. How do you like my wake?"

Paoli opened her eyes. "What did you do to me?" she demanded.

"Don't tell me you can't remember! Lollypop, we did first one thing and another, and then tried some of the better ones all over again."

"You poisoned me!" she accused.

"I did no such thing—" He stopped, studied her face and then said, "*Ah . . .* you've got a hangover. Say, that's too bad. Now me—I've never had a hangover in my life." Owen offered the bottle. "Take a nip of this—it will cure any hangover ever made."

"Go away. You are a poisoner!"

"I am *not.*" Owen was offended. "You just drank too much the first time around, that's all. You don't see *me* poisoned, do you? Of course not—I can handle any old rotgut ever made, and I had twice as much as you did. It won't last, baby doll. Got any aspirin in the house?" He sat down on the bed and ran his hand up and down her leg in friendly fashion. That seldom failed to excite a woman. "Try some of the hair of the dog. It did wonders for me."

The blonde reacted in a startling manner. The blonde kicked him. The blow caught him smartly on the rib cage and knocked him off the bed onto the floor.

"Hey!" he cried in alarm.

"My head is splitting, I am coming apart. I don't want you playing with my leg."

"Well, you don't have to kick me apart to say it."

"Owen Hall, you are a fiend. I despise you!" She put her hands to the sides of her head and moaned. "Your gods are barbarians. *You* are a barbarian."

"Lady, you sure have changed. A couple of hours ago I was the salt of the earth, to hear you tell it—I was the greatest stud ever to come down the pike, to hear you tell it. You *liked* it and you wanted more." Owen spread his hands with despair. "But now look—"

"Leave this house. *Go* somewhere."

Owen picked himself up off the floor but kept a prudent distance between himself and the bed.

"I'm hungry. I was hoping you'd fix supper."

The blonde made a strange strangling sound. Owen watched with a keen interest but then decided that she wasn't really strangling; she was only attempting to scream but the vocal chords weren't cooperating with the desire. He pocketed the friendly bottle and backed away another few steps. If she were able to get to her feet and remain there an appreciable time she might even attack him.

"Go!" she finally managed to cry. "Leave!"

"I guess that means no supper."

Paoli rocked on the bed. She braced her hands behind her back and struggled to sit up, but then abruptly realized it as a rash move and fell back.

Owen was poised for flight. "All right, all right, I can take a hint. There ain't no flies on me. This means our one-night stand is cancelled—this means you're backing down on your promise."

Paoli screamed at him. "I despise barbarians! Get out *now*. Go somewhere. Do *not* come back!" She put her hands over her eyes to shut out the sight of him—and then jerked them away to stare at his clothing. "You are wearing my clothes. Take them off and get out!"

Owen said, "Like hell I will," and broke for the door. There was a sodden sound behind him, as if the angry blonde had tried to roll from the bed and had fallen to the floor. He bolted through the green door.

"My clothes," Paoli cried from behind him.

Owen sped down the walkway without bothering to scan the area for monitors. He ran across the rolling road without losing balance and jumped into the concealing grasses beyond the roadway. Owen hugged the ground and warily watched the open doorway.

After a long while Paoli appeared there, staggering to keep herself upright. She clutched the doorframe and peered hazily up and down the road. By the expression on her face, Owen thought she would be cursing if only she knew the words. He tried to burrow deeper into the grass. There were no more than a dozen workmen in sight, and all of them were wearing the drab coveralls and staring at their feet. It was sunset and the day was nearly done.

The blonde was nearly done. She closed the door and disappeared from Owen's sight. He waited in the grass for a cautious time, but she did not reappear. Owen thought it likely that she had tottered back to bed.

"She didn't even thank me for the new door," he complained aloud. "And after all I did for her, too."

Nine

In every deed of mischief he had a heart to resolve, a head to contrive, and a hand to execute.

—Edward Gibbon

Owen Hall felt like Charlie Chan's number one son, crouching in the grass and watching the road and the many doorways. He was uncomfortably aware that his new pink coveralls exposed his position in the grass if anyone cared to look and that his own drab pair lay on the lawn before Paoli's house like a betraying banner.

He raised his head to scan the ways.

Only one monitor was visible in the distance and her back was to him. Owen climbed up, scampered across the road, and snatched up his discarded clothing. He was back into the concealing grasses within minutes, but this time he fell into a new hiding place farther along, where the road had carried him.

He supposed the fool thing ran all night.

Owen folded the dun-colored coveralls into a loose package and stuffed them into the opening at his waist, buttoning up for safekeeping. The grayish-brown color of the garment would be suitable for midnight skulking. He wormed away from the road for added safety and then stopped to reconnoiter.

The solitary warden was still visible in the remote distance but the road was carrying her toward him. Owen counted bodies. There were eight—no, nine—workmen stretched out in a ragged and disconnected line along the roadway, and as he counted, one of them dropped off to enter a house. The fellow hadn't bothered to knock, and Owen made a note of that. The man had simply swung off the road in a familiar maneuver, shuffled up the short walk to his appointed door, and opened it without sound or signal. Just like the man of the house coming home from a hard day at the salt mines. Owen looked at the empty doorways across the way and at the closed doors near them. He thought it likely that he could do the same, but it wouldn't be smart to enter one of the places having a missing door. The lady of the house just might send him packing—send him right back to the salt mines.

Like Charlie Chan, the world's oldest man had to use his head in perilous times like these.

Owen speculated on his chances of starting a revolution. The town was ripe for revolt—here were all those poor zombies being worked from sunrise to sunset and then made to sleep on a bare cot in the back room, and all without benefit of a water cooler or a restroom at the factory. It was likely that none of them had ever heard of President Roosevelt's Fair Wages and Hours Law, none of them had an inkling of their rights, none of them knew that they were entitled to at least sixty cents an hour for their sweat. Well, no, they didn't sweat, come to think of it, but that was no excuse—they were entitled to a decent wage and only eight hours' work a day, and their rights were being violated on every hand. That kind of treatment bred riots and revolutions, and these poor fellows were ripe for a revolution. Owen thought he was just the man to lead a revolt; he was pretty sharp at bargaining for a fair price, and once he'd served on a grievance committee.

He'd have to give the matter some serious thought. A new approach would be needed—a different approach from the simple one he'd used that morning when urging the factory employees to strike. They hadn't paid any attention to him, of course, but that was because he lacked the proper color of uniform. If he appeared before them while dressed in pink they'd jolly well listen to his orders. He was a commanding figure, given the proper uniform.

He'd once worn an Uncle Sam uniform in the Fourth of July parade in Hartford City, and another time for the Harvest Moon Festival he'd masqueraded as an Apache.

After the revolution, of course, he'd want to choose a suitable position for himself, a responsible place of leadership to the downtrodden masses. The mayor's office might be nice. If there was one thing this town needed—

Owen hastily flopped down into the grass, startled by a sudden glimpse of pink.

A monitor stood with her back to him, staring in open-mouthed astonishment at the gaping doorways. She hopped off the road and took a few hesitant steps across a lawn the better to see the phenomenon. Owen thought he could understand her shock; the word had surely gone all over town of the one missing door earlier in the afternoon, but now there were four. It couldn't be blamed on mice.

The woman walked up to the nearest doorway and peered inside. She called a greeting—or perhaps it was a question—but there was no answer from within. After a minute hesitation she stepped across the sill and went in for an inspection. Owen held his breath and waited. He was fairly certain that all the houses had been empty when he purloined the doors. No one had challenged him.

The puzzled monitor reappeared after a moment and moved on to the adjoining place, where the ritual was repeated. That house was also empty. The questing woman bypassed Paoli's putrid green door (for which Owen was deeply grateful) and went on to investigate the two dwellings beyond hers. Jackpot. Someone answered from the darkened interior of the fourth and last doorless house, and in a moment there were two agitated women standing on the sill debating the loss.

It was almost as much fun as a mud show.

There seemed to be an argument. The occupant of the house was visibly upset, and it appeared to Owen that she was holding the warden personally responsible for the long-gone door. One of the voices was raised in accusation. The other voice vehemently denied the thievery. There was much waving of arms and flapping of hands. The warden stepped away and pointed to the other empty frames nearby. The occupant followed her outside to have a better view and the exchange began anew. A babble of questions and counterquestions ensued. Their voices turned shrill.

In the end both of them took to their heels on the roadway. The road wasn't moving nearly fast enough to carry them wherever they wanted to go, and they broke into a trot to speed their journey. Owen sat up to watch them go. They hurried away to the northeast, to the section of the city he thought of as downtown becuase the factories were there. It was likely that City Hall—if the town had a City Hall—was also located in the downtown area.

Owen seized the opportunity.

He jumped from his hiding place in the grass and dashed across the road to the vacated house. It was as dim as twilight inside, but that presented no problems to an accomplished cat burglar like himself. The floor plan was precisely the same as that of Paoli's apartment.

The dwelling wasn't entirely vacant.

There was nothing on the workbench to interest him; it was cluttered with work shoes and coveralls and the usual instruction books on how to build a man in your own home. The topmost manual was opened to a foldout page, but Owen pointedly ignored that page and ignored a coffin propped up in a corner. The lounging area was as empty as the bedroom, although the bed was rumpled. Owen ran to the rear door to slide the bolt free, then backed off to stare at the workman lying on the cot. The man lay as if dead. His eyes were closed and he appeared to be sleeping, but Owen decided against poking him to find out.

There were two unused candles on the table in the dining area, plus a small metal tube that resembled a woman's lipstick tube and the remains of a half-eaten meal on a plate. Owen scooped up the food to feed his face and recognized the very good bread of the master baker he'd seen at work that morning. The meat was poor horse and wholly unrecognizable—it may have been sorry meatloaf—but the bread was of top quality —the kind found at home rather than in a restaurant. Perhaps it was accidental, but someone had finally found and matched a man to his trade. Owen checked the house a last time, saw nothing more that would be useful to him, and hurried next door to repeat the search.

The lady of that house hadn't yet come home.

He found several candles on the workbench and slipped a couple into his pocket, then looked about for matches. There were none. There was also a refreshing lack of masculine clothing, shoes, manuals, and coffins in the shop. Owen peered into the bedroom, the shower, the kitchen, and into the stiff room at the rear, but all were untenanted. He unlocked the escape route door and ran back to the front. The road was still free of wardens, and he wondered if the two women had run off to get a posse or merely hold a conference at City Hall.

Paoli's door was still shut.

Owen lifted the latch without a betraying sound. The door was slowly inched open. He waited a spell, listened carefully, and then put his head around the door's edge. There were no lights in the love nest, but there was a very pronounced and familiar sound from the vicinity of the bedroom. There was no need to remove his shoes for stealth. Owen went in quietly and stood at the corner of the room divider, marveling at the sight. The blonde was sprawled on the bed as naked as he had left her, making night music. Her lusty snoring would have drowned out any noises he made coming in—it was a healthy, ripsawing after-the-binge snoring. She would thank him in the morning.

"Baby doll, you could audition for Alexander's ragtime band and win. Don Ameche would love you!"

Owen went to the bench to retrieve his matches and cigars, then left the house as quietly as he had entered. The night music went on without stop.

Owen stopped on the walk to scan the road and the distances. It appeared that the whole town went to bed at sundown.

"I *would* make a hell of a good cat burglar—the town is mine for the taking."

The house next to Paoli's had no occupant. It did have the usual think-and-do machine, the usual workbench, and all the common furniture now covered with thick dust, but the total absence of shoes and clothing and tools and candles said that it was empty of living woman and cadaverous workman alike. Owen thought the place would be an excellent base of operations; it offered not only a place to spend the night, but a place of refuge as well. He need only replace the door to give him privacy and fend off the snooping wardens.

He unlocked the rear door and then went out front to scout for a likely replacement.

And ran headlong into the same frustration as before. Doors failed to match frames, being either a quarter- or a half-inch too wide or too narrow to fit.

Owen Hall expressed his opinion of the carpenters who'd done the work, using choice words and phrases known to good old Indiana boys who were extremely vexed. When taxed, Owen could swear like a trooper, and he liked to think that he knew more slang whang than any other man his age. He'd give a pretty penny to know who was responsible for this mess, whether it be workman or woman, and then he'd be willing to give another penny for the opportunity to criticize that culprit to his or her face.

Six useless, shoddy doors were piled on the lawn before the vacant house he'd chosen as a place of refuge; six nearby dwellings hung open to the world. There were no zombies about to tote the damned things home for him, so Owen simply piled the doors onto the roadway and let that marvelous invention carry them away. Perhaps they'd ride round and round the town all night long to surprise the early risers in the morning.

And now there were ten doorless dwellings to confuse the ladies when they returned. That ought to shake up the posse and give them food for thought.

Owen felt so frustrated, so angry that he had a long stiff drink. And then another.

The bottle's contents were running perilously low and he'd have to do something about that when he moved into the empty snuggery. Real soon now. Paoli had said that the power was always on so the think-and-do machine should serve his bidding. It had damned well better.

He shook a screwdriver at the row houses. "One more time! *One* more cotton-picking door, and if *it* doesn't fit, to hell and blazes with it. I'll give the town back to the Indians—they're entitled." He'd sleep in the empty lodgings without the luxury of a door if it came to that, and be damned to the nosy woman who dared peek inside.

Summer darkness was overtaking him. The screws in the hinge holes were difficult to see and he had to feel for the slots with his fingers before inserting the screwdriver. It was tedious work. The door came slowly. It was now too dark to see the color of the thing, but he didn't really care—all he wanted was a decent door to give him privacy for the night.

The last screw came free and he lifted the panel out of the frame.

"Hey—dummy!"

Owen said, "Oh, *God*."

"What are you doing with my door?"

Owen cried, "Firewood," and broke into a run.

The aroused resident thundered after him.

He ran away from the woman, away from the same huge and drunken harridan who had so meanly launched him into the strange new world at sunrise. The behemoth with the sour mash tonsils. The road was rolling in the wrong direction but he wasn't going that way anyhow. Owen raced off in the opposite direction, toward the southwest and Paoli, toward all the empty doorways and all the escape hatches he had arranged.

"Stop, *runt*. Drop that door!"

Owen ran the harder with the door tucked under his arm. The ogre lumbered after him in full bellow.

"Stop the dummy! Somebody stop him. Thief!"

There was a sudden answering cry in the distant darkness ahead and Owen thought that the posse had returned; even now there might be a mob galloping up the road at top lung, intent on his capture. They might even string him up if door thievery was as serious a crime as horse theft.

The behemoth cried, "Come here, dummy! Stop!"

A voice in the darkness ahead answered, "Ho! What is the trouble?"

"The dam has broke," Owen yelled out. "Take to the hills!"

He swerved and darted into the nearest open doorway. The stolen door was set on edge crossways in the opening, a temporary barrier intended to gain him time.

Owen sped to his escape hatch at the rear and leaped through it into the concealing jungle. He was just closing that hatch when the pursuing woman crashed through his frail barrier at the front and sent up an outraged howl. The barrier, at knee level, tripped her. Door and dinosaur fell together in a jumble of thrashing arms and legs, angry bellows, demolished hinges, and shattered wood. The floor shook. It sounded like a rehearsal for doomsday. The furious woman seized the poor remains of her door and wrestled with it, only belatedly realizing that the pulp in her hands was not the wanted man. She hurled the debris aside and climbed to her feet.

"I have the runt now!"

Owen sidled away from the exit, feeling along the ground for the sets of pipes to guide him. He eased along the wall to the next unlocked door and slipped it open.

A candle was being lit in the kitchen. Bellowings of rage were easily heard in the kitchen through the thin separating walls of adjoining apartments.

Owen hastily backed out.

His slow progress along the rear wall continued as another set of pipes signaled yet another dwelling. There was no moon to aid him and he was quickly thankful that the citizens of the town had indoor plumbing rather than backyard privies. This was a poor time to stumble onto a privy in the dark or to fall into the hole where an outhouse had once stood in odorous glory.

Another door opened beneath his fingers.

The house was unlit and lacked the smells and sounds of a tenant. He moved silently through the musty rooms. The cot at the rear was empty of man and the kitchen table was bare of all but dust; the larger bed was uninhabited and the workbench had been swept clean of tools, clothing, and manuals. He was in the vacant house next to Paoli, but now he had no door to hang for his own privacy. It had been a mistake to remove *this* one, but, what the hell, there was no point in crying over spilled milk and splintered doors. The thing would make firewood for somebody.

Owen stared around the interior, seeing dim and nearly formless shapes in the darkness. The opaque room divider before the bed would serve nicely. He hauled the divider to the front of the house, stood it on end and fitted it over the doorframe. It made a splendid barrier. The divider was larger in all dimensions than the missing door and covered the opening with several inches to spare. If he had hammer and nails he could have nailed the barricade in place—there was so much commotion just up the street that the noise of his hammering wouldn't be heard. He pulled two straight chairs and propped them against the barricade to keep it tightly sealed.

A solitary candle burned on his workbench.

Owen Hall very carefully visualized the packsack he'd worn on his weekend fishing trips back there in Indiana. He had supposed that the pack was as familiar as the back of his hand, but now he discovered that he'd taken it for granted. A high order of concentration was called for. The pack had been fashioned of canvas, with padded canvas shoulder straps, a single chest strap, and heavy duty stitching all around. The stitching was important—it wouldn't do for the victuals to fall out the first time he gave rough treatment. There had been two voluminous pockets in the pack, with each held closed by a tie-down. Now, then—had there been any hardware on the packsack? Owen zeroed in on the mental picture. Yes, there *was* hardware: two small brass buckles for fastening the straps after they were adjusted for length. It was funny how he'd used the packsack all those years but had to stop and think of the details now.

He activated the machine and pressed his forehead to the bar. The operating theater lit and delivered.

The pack was identical to the one he'd owned back yonder, even to the stains it had accumulated during long use. Owen examined the stitching carefully and exulted. What fine workmanship! What artistic expression! Why, if he had one of these machines at home he could go into production for all the sports in Indiana, he could sign a supply contract with Sears Roebuck. (But he'd have to remember to omit the stains, of course. The proud new owners of his packs would want to add their own coffee spills and bacon drippings.) Owen was so pleased that he returned to the machine and made a duplicate.

His subconscious reproduced the identical stains.

The matter of supplies was cause for some thought. A traveler could be out on the prairie for a week or more before chancing across a friendly town, but it there were no cattle or buffalo available, a traveler could get hungry. In Hartford City, Juanita's Grocery had provided most of the items he'd taken along on fishing trips, but that small store didn't stock everything necessary for survival, and an occasional trip into Indianapolis was called for. Food for survival. Fishermen and cowboys ate lots of beans and peaches and cornpone, of course, but Owen wanted more than that sparse diet. Cheese, soup, dried fruit, dried peas—maybe even some green beans. He thought he should stock up on pemmican, hard tack, and bullybeef, as well as staples like coffee, salt, and maybe a pinch of sugar. Yes, and butter if he could possibly manage it. With practice he might be able to produce a better spread than the sick axle grease another man had manufactured that morning.

No spinach. Definitely no spinach.

He mustn't forget the essentials like a coffeepot, frying pan, and a couple of can openers. Making quality food neatly tucked away inside cans and jars would be a mite tricky, but he had clear memories of the goods filling the shelves of Juanita's Grocery and that was a definite advantage—that and the skill he'd exhibited earlier in making fine bourbon from memory. He was an artisan.

Owen bellied up to the machine and started work.

He had thought at first that two rucksacks were one too many for his needs, but now he was surprised at how quickly one was filled, and he still hadn't worked his way through his shopping list. The work continued. When an item of food appeared that seemed faulty, Owen subjected it to a taste test. If it was decent after all, he ate it and manufactured another, but if the taste was as poor as the appearance, he cast it aside and tried to improve the item with better visualization. The discovery was made that many foodstuffs of a truly superior quality came out of the operating theater when his taste buds and saliva flow cooperated with his imagination. The second rucksack was filled and Owen called it a night, after remembering to whip up another supply of cigars and a fifth of bourbon. There was always the possibility of snakebite out there on the prairie.

He wondered if he'd forgotten anything.

Yes—by jingo!—he had. He lacked a sturdy hand ax and a good skinning knife. A frontiersman wasn't worthy of the name if he didn't carry an ax and a knife for his survival. Owen made the ax first and pronounced it good after a minute inspection; the ax was as well made and as professionally fashioned as the carpenter's tools he'd turned out that morning. Owen modestly admitted that he was a master craftsman. The knife came next, but the first sample was a sorry one. Owen paused, carefully visualized a rack of knives seen in a sporting goods store, selected one that he fancied, and put his head to work. The machine delivered a highly satisfactory instrument.

He tucked both knives, the ax, and the bottle of whiskey into the rucksacks, tied everything down, and set the gear at the foot of the bed for the morning. It would be wise to get a few hours' sleep while the posse scoured the town, and then slip away to the woods before daylight. The candle was pinched out.

Owen padded to the front door to reconnoiter.

He pried open a finger-sized slit at one side of the divider and peered out.

It was an astounding scene.

The posse was there—eight or ten tall women zooming up and down before all the doorless houses like a swarm of bees without a leader. They ran about, gesturing and yelping. The ham-handed harridan was there— the woman who had first made him and then turned against him; she stood on the walk waving her large arms and crying for the blood of the dummy. And some of the missing doors had come home to roost—some of the doors had ridden all the way around the city and now here they were again, being taken off the road and stacked on a lawn. A warden stood over them with screwdriver in hand.

Owen wished her luck.

He searched for the source of the illumination.

The women weren't behaving like bees, they were more like flitting fireflies. Owen stared at their torches and fell back in new astonishment. Torches! He hastily closed the makeshift door. The wardens carried hand-held torches just like those people in old movies—the frenzied villagers who had assaulted Frankenstein's castle. *That* was the source of the light outside.

He shook his head in dismay. There wasn't a genius in the town who had the wit to invent electricity (putting himself aside, of course). They had futuristic machines that could reproduce anything a man or woman dreamed of, they had a mechanical road right out of the science-wonder magazines, and somewhere in the town they must have a giant rubber-band factory to power that road, but they lacked the wit to invent flashlights, wires, and light bulbs.

"It's a rum place," he said again. "The Indians wouldn't take it back unless you bribed 'em with scalps."

There was an authoritative knock at the door.

Owen knew it was time to skedaddle—his sleep and his snuggery were lost. He grabbed up the two rucksacks and headed for the escape hatch. The knock came again, this time more demanding. Owen was through the rear portal and out into the weeds before the divider was pushed aside.

Where was a refuge?

The doll's house was nearby. Owen crawled over the pipes and set down his twin burdens at the tradesman's entrance. The door was eased open and he listened for the familiar snoring. Surprise. The tall blonde was no longer sleeping or snoring. She was standing at the front arguing with another woman—a stranger—over the door a kindly carpenter had so recently hung. The stranger was upset and demanding her door back. Paoli was angry at being awakened and equally angry at the suggestion that *she* was a conspirator to the plot. Her tone and her manner betrayed the state of her head, and Owen guessed that she hadn't found aspirin for the hangover.

He closed the hatch silently and backed away. Geez, the whole neighborhood was in an uproar. You'd think that the cops had found a fifth columnist in the act of poisoning the reservoir.

Owen shouldered one of the packsacks and adjusted the straps for a comfortable fit. The other pack would have to be carried in arm as he struck off into the weedy wilderness in search of a hideout. All his thoughtful work in unbolting the hatches was for naught—if the cops had roused Paoli, they'd roused everybody, and if those other ladies were only half as vexed as Paoli, they'd be loathe to offer him supper and solace.

Owen prided himself on the ability to take a hint, however subtle. It was past time to beat a retreat.

Ten

"Blonde or dark, sir?"
says enough
Whether of women, drink,
or snuff.

—Robert Graves

Owen Hall sat on a pipe, swinging his heels and munching a homemade biscuit. The manhunters were getting the smarts.

He had worked his slow way about an eighth of a mile through the tangle of weeds and pipes, first moving straight inland toward the powerhouse at the city's center and then turning sharply northeast toward downtown but away from the agitated villagers. When he judged that he was safely away from them in the concealing darkness, he rested the packs, dug out a biscuit, and climbed atop a pipe to watch the turmoil. The sky still lacked a moon and that was to his advantage.

If the bustling wardens weren't more careful they'd set fire to the row houses.

A solitary woman brandishing a torch had been the first to appear out back. She popped through one of the exits Owen had unlatched for himself and scanned the dark ways to either side, seeking the culprit. The torch was lifted on high as the warden peered into the depths of the weeds. Owen sat unmoving. The poor light of the torch wouldn't reveal him at an eighth of a mile. The

122

woman faced about and studied the doors along the back wall, then called a question into the house she had just left. There was no answer, and she went back inside. Owen waited. In the next few moments several of his hatches were thrown open and the posse erupted in full cry. It had taken them that long to recognize his escape route.

Owen spotted Paoli at her door looking out on the hubbub. She seemed less than happy.

The scene again suggested fireflies dancing on a summer night. The fireflies came together in a group. Somebody organized a search, somebody came up with a plan that might have worked *if* he were still inside and *if* they had remembered to guard all the front doors. A warden was stationed at each doorway opening onto the weed patch, while two others with torches went inside to conduct a room-by-room search of the house. When that place was found to be empty of the fugitive, the searchers went next door to repeat the investigation. The wardens probed Paoli's house, much to her dismay, and then the two houses beyond. When they came upon a locked door, they reversed themselves and worked up the line of row houses toward the harridan's dwelling. That woman stood waiting for them with huge arms folded belligerently across her chest. Owen was reminded of a female wrestler he'd seen at a stag party in Indianapolis—the wrestler who had played the villain's role.

Owen thought the zealous monitors were overdoing it a bit. He hadn't removed that many front doors or unbolted that many rear hatches, but, what the hell, Jack, if they were happy in their work, give them an E for effort and let them fly the flag atop City Hall. A town took pride in the number of E flags they had flying.

The fat-bellied leviathan set up a clamor when they finally reached her door but, as best as Owen could judge, she wasn't saying anything new. The voice was shrill and angry, but the vocabulary was a disappointment. Given her temper and her forty-odd years of life, the witch should have accumulated enough crusty cusswords to fill a honey bucket. She trailed the wardens through her door, complaining all the way—but Owen was willing to bet **that** she never admitted to being responsible for him.

The door next to hers was suddenly opened and yet

another curious neighbor popped out to learn the cause of the commotion. Owen sat up with pleased surprise.

The newcomer was Kehli, the brown-eyed, brown-haired mistress of the gravediggers.

Kehli had said that she was a near neighbor of Paoli's, but she hadn't mentioned being even closer to the loud-mouthed ogre. Owen watched Kehli until the wardens came back empty-handed, and everybody gathered for a conference.

He slid off the pipe and made ready to crawl or take to his heels. The rucksacks were tucked under the largest pipe to avoid discovery.

The frustrated wardens were in a huddle beneath the massed torches, and their next line of action would depend on their imaginations or the belated realization of what they had failed to do. Owen waited, poised for flight. The complaining woman was stomping around them, waving those great hands. An Indiana cop would have shut her mouth in a hurry.

"Hot damn, they forgot! As sure as a weasel sucks eggs, they forgot to watch the front!"

The pack of huddled monitors broke in unison and again raced through the nag's house with that woman hard on their heels—and the whole silly charade began anew. Owen crawled back atop the pipe to watch the show and found the audience of two were still with him. Paoli watched the antics from the far end of the arena and Kehli watched from the near end, his end. He counted the pipes nearby and noted the set that served her house.

The forces of law and order fashioned an artful drag-net to catch a slyboots. On this second mad go-around a warden stood guard at each of the doors, fore and aft, as they should have done at the beginning to prevent the fugitive from sneaking out the back as the pursuers entered the front, or to prevent him from skulking house by house just ahead of the dragnet, or to prevent him from doubling back and finding refuge in a place already swept clean. Slyboots approved of their acumen. It was a splendid maneuver by a fledgling police force only now learning to cope with their first crime wave, but the fledgling force realized the tardiness of their ways long before the search was completed to the last house.

They went into another huddle.

The dragnet had failed, the fugitive had eluded them once again. He was probably now long gone, over the road and into the trees—or else up the road and into the house of some innocent sleeping citizen. The wardens dispersed, tidying up their police detail by closing and bolting all the escape hatches. Darkness closed in once again. Paoli went indoors. Owen turned back to Kehli just as she was closing and locking her door. Even the terrible-tempered ogre had gone.

There were no returning sounds of crickets or night birds—there was only a dim sky glow that his grandfather used to call the zodiac light. He was alone.

Owen Hall was a clever man, quick to catch a nuance or read a sign. He was locked out—or rather locked *in,* inside the city ring. A pity he hadn't thought to make a ladder for a daring escape over the rooftops.

Owen bided his time for an hour in the suspicion that the pink arms of the law might double back on him. He didn't want to be caught near the row houses if the posse should suddenly erupt through any of the doors.

Jupiter served as his timepiece.

He was fairly certain that he'd owned a wristwatch and fairly certain that he'd been wearing it that night when he met up with the Pennsy freight, but he hadn't had one when he rejoined the world early this morning. Maybe the undertaker had stolen it. No matter. An old woodsman who read the science-wonder magazines had little need for a mechanical watch when the planets were in the sky. Jupiter or Saturn had served him well on many a nighttime fishing or camping expedition and now, with Jupiter just rising above the eastern rooftops, it was no problem to mark off an hour.

There was something funny about the stars though. The old familiar ones weren't quite where they were supposed to be, and some of the configurations were—well, odd.

Owen stood on the topmost pipe to gain a better view over the rooflines.

For starters, something peculiar had happened to the Big Dipper. It appeared flatter than he remembered it and more open; the dipper itself now couldn't hold nearly as much water as before, and the handle was twisted out of shape. And another thing—there were supposed to be eight stars in the formation, but now he could count only seven. He had prided himself on his sharp eyesight in the old days—he'd always been able to separate the double star in the dipper's handle—but that double wasn't visible now. Either the faint companion star had simply vanished from the sky or the woman who had reconstituted him last night had skimped on his eyeballs.

The polestar just wasn't believable.

Owen went back to the Big Dipper for orientation, poor as it was, and then attempted to track an imaginary path across the sky from the Dipper's lip to Polaris. The path failed to track straight; it refused to make the familiar connection. He found the Little Dipper with some difficulty (something had happened to it, too) and traced the handle northward to Polaris at the tip end—but Polaris wasn't at the end where it should be. It had moved, or been pushed. Polaris was now over *there*, off the handle. (If an outdoorsman couldn't trust the polestar, what *could* he trust?) The sky was confusing.

Owen sat down to puzzle the matter. He dug another biscuit out of his pack.

If only his memory was keener, if only all the empty little recesses of his past life could be filled in, an answer might be found. It was frustrating to have holes in his head. The Chicago *Tribune* had published scores of scientific articles on scores of Sundays in his time, and the science-wonder magazines were always chattering about the future, but what had they said about the movements of the stars in times to come? There was a vague memory of something—something about Thurban having been the polestar five or six thousand years ago and about Vega becoming the polestar some twelve thousand years in the future—but confound it, the memory was too vague.

Drat! that drunken woman who'd made him. She not only skimped on his eyeballs, but she omitted some gray cells as well.

He looked over his shoulder to the north, studying Polaris again. There was the notion in mind that he might have been buried for five hundred or a thousand years, but could Polaris have moved *that* far in only five hundred or a thousand years? It didn't seem likely. Something had to be altered. Either the two Dippers had changed and the polestar had jumped a country mile in a thousand years, or he'd been underground much longer than supposed.

Two thousand years? *Three* thousand? Why, that was fantastic. Of course, his bones could last as long as any old Egyptian king's, but that was fantastic.

Every time he thought he had it figured, every time he was sure the situation was well in hand, something else came along to upset the apple cart. It was disconcerting. The *least* these women could do was have a calendar that a man could rely on—a calendar beginning with the big war—say, in 1939, when it really started—and working right up to today—his first day of his new life. A man would know at a glance how long he'd been out of circulation. A man could sit and figure the amount of his pension. The present situation was utterly ridiculous; nobody knew nothing, and what was a man left with? He was left holding a bucket of rancid chicken fat, that's what.

If he ever got back to Indiana, he'd write a letter to President Roosevelt about this sorry state of affairs. The President might want to mention it in his next fireside chat.

Owen glanced at Jupiter and calculated that his hour of margin had passed. The planet was well above the rooftops, but there was still no sign of a moon. He finished the biscuit in hand, gathered up his gear, and followed a set of pipes to Kehli's door. As a test he first tried the doors to either side of his goal and found them both bolted. There was little point in testing any of the others, since they would all be the same. The loud-mouthed posse would have alerted everybody up and down the length of Main Street by this time.

Owen knocked boldly on the lady's door and waited. The wait was so long that he was beginning to wonder if he'd have to take the thing off its hinges or kick it open to gain admittance. Owen was raising his hand to knock again when it swung outward. He wore a big smile.

"Greetings, skate. Let's congregate."

Kehli stared at him with speechless wonder. She peered around and beyond him.

"Come on, now, remember me? I'm your favorite picnic guest."

She seemed unable to speak.

"Cupcake, it's *me,* Owen Hall. I've brought the party over to your house. Paoli pooped out early on." He bounced through the open door and hauled the packs in after him, forcing the woman to move or be bowled over. "Are you in the party mood? What's for supper?"

Incredulously: "What . . . what were you doing out there?"

"Watching the parade," Owen replied. He stacked his gear against the wall. "I had a ringside seat, and that's how I found you. Good thing you stepped out to take a look—I didn't know your house number."

"You are wearing—" She gestured at the clothing. "Why are you wearing . . . ?"

"I'm wearing Paoli's gladrags. Mine got wet, you see, and I put them out on the grass to dry, but what with one thing and another I had to make these do. It's a long story, cupcake. Now, what about supper?"

"I've eaten my evening meal."

Pointedly: "I haven't."

Her confusion continued and Owen guessed it was caused by his unexpected appearance at her back door. He studied her face, attempting to read beyond the confusion, and suddenly wondered if there was room for a suspicion. She surely didn't have *another* reason for— He stepped around her and peered into the back room, but there was no male waiting on the cot. The kitchen was empty but for a couple of candles burning on the table. Owen felt reassured.

He reached for her hands and held them in a firm, friendly grip. She was startled but didn't pull away. He drew her into the kitchen.

"Kelly, a lot of things happened this afternoon and we had a bang-up blanket party, Paoli and me. Oh, we had a lovely wake! First, Paoli got plastered and fell off the chair, and then she got her clothes dirty in the oven, and then we went into the shower to clean up, and after that we stepped outside for a breath of air, and then—well, cupcake, we did just what comes naturally. The dolly was impressed."

"Paoli was looped? Flying the kite?"

"And how!" He pulled the bottle from his pocket to exhibit the remaining contents. "She really appreciates the good stuff, and you can read that two ways."

Kehli seemed equally impressed. Astonished, but impressed. "And did you . . . did you . . . ?"

"Yup. With bells on. Paoli had this hankering to see what a good ol' Indiana variant could do when the flag went down, so I did my best." Owen paused to reflect on his modest accomplishments. "Hoo boy, did I ever deliver the telegram! Sort of surprised myself, I did, but then I never met a woman like Paoli before. Are all the women here like her? Are you?"

"I . . . I cannot answer that."

"Well, Kelly, what I'm getting at is this: we were *so* busy, *so* long, and she was *so* tired afterward that we never did get around to fixing supper. She just wanted to sleep, but that's natural, see? Now me, I'm starving." He watched her face and decided it was very nice to see a woman blush by candlelight.

"You are not willing to wait until morning?"

"I can't. Cupcake, I said *starving*."

"It is too late. Evening meals are no longer being served because it is late. Only the morning breakfasts will be available."

Desperately: "I *like* breakfast!" Visions of succulent bacon danced through his head. "Make it a double order and ask for some grits while you're at it. Lots of whole wheat toast and grape jam, but no butter. I don't trust that guy's butter. Do you people know what coffee is around here?"

"I have not heard of coffee."

The woman pulled free of his grasp and went to a box fitted into the kitchen wall. The contraption reminded Owen of an oven once again—an oven made of dark gray metal resembling pig iron. The box lacked a glass door for sighting, but it had a handle at the top and the usual row of buttons underneath. He supposed it was on the receiving end of one of those outside pipes—perhaps the large one he thought of as a furnace pipe.

Kehli ordered up his breakfast by push button.

"Now you're cooking with gas, cupcake."

Nothing happened immediately and the brown-haired woman leaned against the wall to wait.

"What's holding up the show?" he demanded.

"Be patient. The food must be delivered and then this unit must heat it."

"Right out of the old bean factory," Owen nodded. "In some ways you babes have got this town organized to a fare-thee-well, but in other ways you fall flat on your faces. Just like the bureaucrats back home."

"I am not understanding you again."

"Who does, around this town?" He liked the way her brown hair curled down over the pink-clad shoulders. The gravedigger was a lovely woman. "I'd be pleased to teach you American if I stay around, Kelly. We could make beautiful music together."

"But you will not stay around to teach, Owen Hall. You must be reconstructed to eliminate the defects."

He eyed her with quick concern. "You too, eh?"

"I am too what?"

"Never mind—but thanks for the warning. I'll keep my guard up."

A signal bell sounded above the oven and Kehli opened the door to retrieve his breakfast, steaming hot and ready for serving. Owen moved up beside her and peered around her arm when he found that he couldn't peer over her shoulder.

The woman seemed stunned. She made no move to reach in for the meal.

Owen stared at a broiled monkey wrench. The wooden handle was done to a crisp.

"Son of a gun! The turkey is home to roost."

She cried with dismay, *"What is that?"*

"A monkey wrench. What did you think it was—a nutcracker?"

"But where . . . *where* did it come from?"

"From the bean factory, where else?" He inspected the smoldering handle with disapproval. "I'd send it back if we were eating in a fancy, expensive restaurant."

She whirled away from the oven and Owen took a prudent step backward.

"Did you do that?"

"Guilty, your honor."

"That is why the processing plant was shut down— *that* is why the workmen were sent home early."

"I thought it was the union hours."

"Owen Hall, do you realize what you have done to the city?" Kehli seemed on the brink of tears and that purely surprised him; he didn't know that amazons ever cried. "Do you realize that people may go hungry tomorrow?"

"I'm going hungry tonight," he reminded the woman. "There goes my supper unless you push the buttons again."

"How many of those . . . things did you make?"

"Just one," he said truthfully. "That one."

"Owen Hall, you are a totally irresponsible variant. I fear your maker will be punished."

"She ought to be strung up by her thumbs," Owen responded. "Do you want to meet her? You'll be sorry."

"Was not Paoli your fabricator?"

"Paoli was not my fabricator. *She* didn't make me, cupcake, I made her. That's a joke." He waggled a finger at the adjoining wall to indicate the apartment next door. "Fatstuff, in there, made me. Didn't you leave a coffin on her doorstep yesterday?"

Kehli's surprised glance followed the finger.

She asked, "Hoon?"

"Hoon, goon. *Did* you leave a coffin over there?"

"Yes."

"Well, there you are." He spread his hands. "You dug me up and a drunken goon put me together. Guess whose fault I am, and guess what that's got to do with the price of pancakes in Albania. Are you going to push the buttons again? My belly's growling like a possum in heat."

"I cannot do that, Owen Hall. It is impossible."

"Why is it impossible?"

"I have used my breakfast allotment for tomorrow. There will be no more until the day after."

"Kelly—is this town being rationed too? There ain't no war on here. Are you dames on ration?"

"Each of us is permitted one breakfast a day. There cannot be two."

Owen looked at the monkey wrench waiting in the oven. "You spent your rations on *me*. Kelly, I can't let you go hungry—*I* don't want to go hungry."

She was distressed. "But there is nothing more to be done."

"Like hell there ain't." He tapped his chest with a thumb. "Just leave it to the old scout, Kelly."

He took her hand gently and led her to the table and the waiting chair, to the precise center of the table as befitted the hostess. As always she was surprised at his touch but went along willingly. The candles were positioned so that they framed her face—one to either side —and then he brought in another chair and sat down opposite. Owen thought it a romantic setting. His companion was strikingly beautiful by candle flame. The house was entirely dark but for the room they occupied, and if only he knew how to make a radio, they could have soft music as well. Maybe he could hum. Owen smiled at her between the candles and winked his left eye.

"You look elegant, Kelly. My grandfather always said brown-eyed women were best."

She did not reply. The brown eyes watched him.

"Now then, I've got some serious questions and I'd like some serious answers. I'm working up a surprise for you, cupcake. Why do you order food through the pipes? Why do you rely on pushing those buttons yonder?"

"That is how our food is obtained." She was patient. "It is fabricated in the zone and stored until needed."

Owen was skeptical. "I've *seen* the food put together in the zone—uh, downtown, and it's for the birds. Some of the bread and some of the bacon was good stuff, grade A, and I guess the eggs are all right, but the other stuff was bird food. Kelly, it was poor horse."

"I am not familiar with a poor horse."

"Don't bet on it. I ate most of your picnic lunch this morning, remember? And sure enough, the bread was a winner but the meat was shoe leather—stringy shoe leather. There was a jar of funny yellow stuff that could pass for glue, and maybe it was, and some apples that wouldn't fool a dimwitted worm." He waved his hand over the table. "I can tell you what you had for supper tonight. I don't know what you call it, but I call it meatloaf, and it tasted like silage. Kelly, why do you put up with that junk?"

"Not all of the workmen are skilled processors. We teach them as best we can."

"Why in the hell don't you make your own grub?" He pointed toward the front. "You've got a perfectly good creation machine right there in the workshop."

"Oh, *no*, Owen Hall. That machine isn't designed to produce food, it is used for reconstituting recoveries."

Owen peered at the woman between the candles. How did an Indiana gentleman tell a lady that she was dumb —not only wrong but dumb to boot? Grandfather had never given him advice on that subject.

He asked, "Does it make shoes?"

"No."

"Clothing?"

"No."

"Candles?"

"No."

"Only the walking stiffs?"

"Ambulatory recoveries."

Owen shook his head with dismay, knowing that he had missed the boat earlier in the day. Too late, he *knew* how to bring the town to its knees and get himself elected to City Hall. If he could have organized a general strike or mounted a successful revolution, if he could have pulled the men away from their machines, the high-and-mighty pink ladies would be starving in a week's time. The man who controlled the food supply was king of the hill.

"Kelly, I just lost City Hall, but now I'm going to contribute to your education, and believe you me, the pleasure is mine. What do you say to a steak? A tender, juicy steak just oozing with vitamins and goodness?"

She looked puzzled. "What is—"

"Stop!" He put up a quick hand to shut off the question. "I don't believe it! Talk about a rum bunch of numbskulls. Kites, jugs, cigars, dates, horses, cows, steaks, steers—nobody knows *nothing* around here. Nobody but me, that is. Cupcake, you're being robbed."

"But nothing has been taken from me."

"You never had it in the first place. Somebody around here is holding out on you."

"I fail to understand you, Owen Hall."

"Doesn't everybody?"

"I fail to understand—"

"Sshhh." He put a finger to his lips. "Meditation time. A top-notch surprise coming up, cupcake."

Owen put his elbows on the table and propped his head in his hands to think. After a while his eyes closed of their own volition, because he could think better that way. The house was silent. The woman sat quietly across the table and waited on him, not understanding what he was doing but being willing to wait him out.

Texas Tommy's Steak House on Route 31, at the north edge of Indianapolis.

Texas Tommy was no longer there, of course; he had gone over the border into Canada in the autumn of 1939 and enlisted in the Princess Pat Regiment at Windsor or Toronto or one of those places where they accepted Americans with make-believe Canadian addresses. Texas Tommy said he wanted to whip the Hun. By and by, his regiment was shipped overseas to Britain, and for all anyone knew, Texas Tommy was over there yet whooping it up with the English women or battling the Boche, but his steak house was still open and still at the same old stand on Route 31. Texas Tommy's wife was running the place now—leastwise, she claimed to be his wife and nobody questioned it, just as nobody questioned the living arrangements enjoyed by the cook while Tommy was away. It was the kind of restaurant that brought in the swells from the northeast side on Sunday nights, and everybody knew that Texas Tommy's wife raised the price by fifty cents on those nights because the swells had money to burn.

Texas Tommy's steaks were worth more than the price charged for them; they were mouth-watering.

Owen opened his eyes. "Do you have dishes?"

"I have a plate and a glass."

He closed his eyes. Texas Tommy's plates were large ones; a pale yellow color as he remembered them, having red and brown cross stripes reaching to the four points of the compass. A pottery in Ohio made them on special order. The plates were large enough to accommodate a king-sized steak, a baked potato, and generous helpings of corn or peas or beets or green beans or whatever was on the menu that week. There were cups and saucers in a matching pattern, a tall water glass, clean silverware, a very sharp steak knife, and a cloth napkin. That last was important: a cloth napkin. The steaks were delivered to the table exactly as ordered, the vegetables were hot, a pot of coffee was left on the table, the bread plate had both white and whole wheat, and nobody asked if the cup of butter came off the black market. There was cake or pie or ice cream for dessert, and in season strawberry shortcake or watermelon was available. All in all, it was a most satisfying meal for a dollar and a half, and nobody ever heard a swell complain on Sunday night when he was nicked for two dollars.

Owen opened his eyes to look across the table.

"Butter or sour cream on the potato?"

"What—"

"Sour cream," Owen decided. "Kelly, I'm working on the menu, I'm going to fix a supper like you never had in your life—all thirty years of your life. You'll thank me in the morning."

"I think you are making a joke, Owen Hall."

"I am not making a joke Owen Hall, I am making like a gourmet chef. A chef is a kind of fancy cook who gets better wages." He got up and reached across the table for her hand. "Come along up front. I'm going to teach you something. I'm going to show you what that retread machine can *really* do when a genius is at the controls."

The woman went along with him, her hand tucked inside his. "Do you intend to prepare a meal *here?*"

"I intend to prepare a meal here. I intend to show you what you're missing and how somebody downtown is robbing you. Start asking questions tomorrow."

"It cannot be done. Ask what questions?"

"Watch me do it, chop-chop. Ask why you're being fed shoe leather and silage day in and day out, ask why you can't fix your own meals at home on this here machine. Get snotty about it. Throw your weight around. Make them squirm until they come up with honest answers. And when you *do* start cooking at home, let those poor stiffs alone in the graveyard—they got rights too."

"I really don't understand your thought processes, Owen Hall. You speak strangely."

"That's a polite way of saying you think I'm crazy. All right, cupcake, just stand by and watch a crazy man operate, and don't drop the hot plates when they come out of the oven."

"Why are you suddenly behaving like this?"

Owen turned and looked up into her face. He fancied that the distant candles created a halo effect behind her head, enriching the soft brown hair.

"Because I ate your picnic lunch, because you gave me your breakfast and now you have nothing, because you've never had a civilized meal in your life . . . and I think I'm falling in love, Kelly."

Eleven

The appearance of a single great genius is more than equivalent to the birth of a hundred mediocrities.

—Cesare Lombroso

Owen Hall put a napkin to his mouth when he burped because it wasn't polite to do otherwise with a lady at the table. The lady seemed not to notice. He poured himself a final cup of coffee and laced it with a generous slug of bourbon, but Kehli received only two teaspoons of booze in her last cup. Owen didn't want her to follow Paoli down the primrose path to debauchery.

"Why did you do that?" she asked.

"It's the right way to end a meal, the poor man's B and B. Four out of five doctors recommend it."

"Will I like it?"

"Did you like the steak? The chocolate cake?"

"Oh, yes!"

"Then finish up your green beans. Tidy up."

She looked at her plate with a tiny frown. "I am very full in the stomach, Owen Hall."

"Think of all the starving kids in Armenia."

"What is—"

"This is your last meal until you learn to cook for yourself, cupcake. I won't be around tomorrow to do it for you." Owen used a slice of bread to clean the last of the

gravy off his plate, country style. "Remember how everything looked and felt and tasted—this is the only cooking
lesson you'll get from me. I'll wash up the dishes and the
silverware and you can stash them away somewhere, but
you'll have to make your own belly timber. There's five
hundred other things that can be fixed and eaten but I
haven't got that much time left—I can't show you the
full menu." He popped the gravied bread into his mouth,
carefully wiped his lower lip with an index finger and
then waggled that finger at the woman. "Don't forget to
pass the word up and down the street—show those other
broads how to cook for themselves. Let them know how
they're being robbed."

Kehli ate the remaining green beans one at a time.

She hadn't liked the first taste of the beans and the
sampling of a pickle had caused her mouth to pucker and
her eyes to water, but eventually her plate was picked
clean. Her positive appreciation of the sirloin steak had
brought joy to Owen's heart and a boost to his ego; he
thought it likely that he would have been hired on the
spot if Texas Tommy had been present to inspect the
steaks. He could move to Indianapolis and settle down in
a comfortable job.

Kehli had revealed a familiarity with the baked potato
but not with the sour cream filling; she had looked with
wonder at each of the vegetables before tasting them,
while the hot coffee and the slice of chocolate cake had
created an expression often seen on the faces of children
at circus parades. Owen admitted that he was pretty
good.

She sat back from the table and laced her fingers
across her stomach, looking at him with awe.

"I have *never* eaten this much."

"You've never had the chance. Satisfied?"

"It was excellent. Were you a chef cook?"

"Nope, just a journeyman carpenter, but what the hell,
Kelly, if you can make a monkey wrench you can bake a
cake. If you dames were really on the ball, you'd give
those zombies some brains and find out what they can
do." He waggled the admonishing finger again. "Mind
you, I *don't* approve of you digging up those guys at all.
It's positively indecent, and you wouldn't need them if
you'd learn to use your heads. As for those stiffs already
up and walking around, put them to good use and give

them a decent living—find out which of them are cooks or carpenters or zeppelin pilots. You'd be surprised, Kelly."

"I think I am beyond surprises."

Owen grinned wickedly at her. "Cupcake, you are as green as grass. Putty in my hands."

She made no reply but continued to watch him with a newfound interest that bordered on fascination. Her eyes were very large in the dim light.

Owen searched his pockets for an after-dinner cigar and lit it with one of the candles. The taste and quality of the cigar was no better than those he'd smoked during the day and he had to ruefully admit that he wasn't an expert at everything—not *everything*.

Owen blew smoke at the ceiling. "I haven't seen any matches around the town. How do you light the candles?"

Kehli reached into a pocket and gave him what appeared to be a tube of lipstick. Owen examined it with curiosity.

"I saw one of these in somebody's kitchen down the road. What's—oh, *hell*, yes!" He twisted off the cap and found the working end of a cigarette lighter. It was of a design he'd not seen before in either of his lives, but there was no mistaking the object or its purpose. The lighter lacked a flint and a wick and had nothing more than a pinpoint hole at the business end, but it produced a blue flame nearly an inch in length when he rotated an operating disc set into the bottom of it.

"You found this in somebody's grave, didn't you?"

"It was taken from an excavation several years ago. We did not believe it to be an offering to the ancient gods, so we copied it for our own use. Everyone in the city has copies of the artifact."

"*You* found it?"

"I am the only excavator at present."

"I'd like to have one. Do you have an extra for me?"

"You may keep that one, Owen Hall."

"Well, thanks, cupcake, you're a brick." He played with the lighter, watching the steady flame. "I'd give a buffalo nickel to find out how it works. It doesn't use lighter fluid—there's no smell here at all." He sniffed at the orifice after the flame was put out. "How long has it lasted you?"

"It has been at least ten years since the discovery. That is the original, not a copy."

Owen stared at the lighter with amazement. "Ten years without a refill. Imagine that! It's got to be from the future, from nineteen eighty-four or two thousand eighty-seven or one of those years. We never had nothing like this."

"I am pleased that you find it useful."

Owen sipped at his coffee and worked on the cigar. "How come you're the only gravedigger? It's a lousy job, I'll grant you, but how come you have to do all the work?"

"The others are fearful of the wilderness. I am not afraid."

"What wilderness?" He stared across the table.

"The forest and the great open lands—all of that area beyond the excavations is wilderness."

Owen blinked at the woman. "Kelly, that isn't— Well, I guess we've just got different names for the same thing. You call it a forest—I call it a stand of timber, small woods. What you call a wilderness, I call prairie. Farmland the sodbusters haven't discovered yet. It's wild, all right, but not the way you think. People around here are afraid of it, eh?"

"I am not afraid. I am the only one in the city who will supervise the excavations or go into the forest. The others are too fearful of the burial grounds and the wilderness—they mistrust the forest."

"I saw a couple of wardens out there this afternoon. They'd been out to the graveyard hunting me, and when I saw them they were hot-footing it back to town. That means running, coming in along the trail on the double."

"They were running because of their fear of the wilderness."

"Geez," Owen said with mild wonder. "And they were grown women, too." He lifted his coffee cup and prompted Kehli to do the same. "Here's a toast." He touched his cup to hers. "Cheers to a bold dolly."

"Thank you, Owen Hall. I think that is a compliment."

"It purely is, cupcake. I'm a keen judge of women and horses." He watched with an expert's eye while she sampled the laced coffee. It appeared to meet her approval. "Do you get to keep the souvenirs?"

"I don't understand you once more."

"Do you get to keep what you find out there? You found this lighter and I found that yellow ring this morning, but outside of that, do you find a lot of things in the graves? Do they let you keep what you find?"

"The artifacts!" She flashed him a smile. "I will show you."

Kehli rose from the table and went to the workbench at the front. Owen turned his head to watch her go because he admired flowing lines. She was back in a moment with a box full of booty. Owen gasped at the box and its contents and quickly pushed aside the dishes to make room. He spilled the booty out on the table between them.

It was a strange treasure trove—one that would have delighted an archaeologist. The foremost object was also the largest—a dirty gray skull with a bullet hole through the back of the cranium.

"Bushwhacked!" Owen exclaimed. "This poor fellow was bushwhacked."

Kehli's troubled glance passed from the skull to Owen. "He was slain. Did the ancients slay one another for ceremonial purposes?"

"They did it for every reason you can think of, and some you can't. We called it civilization, Kelly." Owen turned the skull about to examine the features, then looked at the woman's expression. "You're shocked. I guess you don't have murder in this here paradise."

"Certainly not! I have never heard of such a thing."

"Lucky you. Don't invent it."

He put the skull aside and poked through the booty with his finger. There were a score or more gold teeth and gold fillings, several war medals, full dentures and partial dentures, a double handful of rings, women's bracelets and necklaces, spectacles with wire frames and spectacles with steel frames, a nose ring, and a dirt-encrusted pocket watch.

"Kelly, you could open a pawnshop."

"What—"

"Skip it, and drink your coffee before it gets cold."

Owen returned his attention to the pocket watch. It was no dollar dummy but instead a fine and expensive timepiece lovingly crafted by some artisan. He soaked a corner of his napkin with whiskey and briskly rubbed the watch to clean away the grime. It appeared to be gold and appeared to be half familiar. A thumbnail found the catch and the lid was lifted away from the glass-covered face. The hinge was stiff from disuse. Time had stopped at eight minutes past three. A short broken length of gold chain hung from the tiny handle crowning and protecting the stem. There was no watch fob among the booty. It was a fine watch and a costly one, designed either for a robber baron or a gentleman.

Owen rubbed the inside of the lid, the better to read an inscription there.

"Is it a religious object?" Kehli asked. "Did the ancients pray by it?"

"Nope, it's a timepiece, and they swore by it. Mind you, sometimes they swore at it. You should have heard the ruckus when President Roosevelt changed the whole country over to daylight saving time to help the war effort. Hoo boy, did some people bitch and moan! There was a joker down there in some backwater Tennessee town who took a hammer to his watch—he really did. He stood out in the middle of the street at high noon and smashed it to smithereens. He claimed that *nobody* had the right to tinker with God's time, and if the President was going to change things around, he refused to be a part of it. He refused to carry Roosevelt time. So he smashed his watch with a hammer and got his picture in the papers."

"It seems to be an odd behavior."

"Tennessee people are full of odd behavior. They ain't like me and you, cupcake."

Cupcake sipped the coffee and watched Owen with contentment.

"I've come across a few of these pieces in my time—two or three of them, I guess. My grandfather carried one almost all of his life until one day he dropped it in the cistern. A cistern is a hole in the ground that holds rainwater," he explained before she could ask. "Rainwater is soft and is best for baths and doing the washing and things like that. Grandfather had a pump in his kitchen and used it for drinking too. He was pretty upset about losing that watch in the cistern.

"And there was another guy, a professor over at Ball State, who carried one. He was a funny little duck. I had a job remodeling his front porch and that old professor would stand around outside watching me work and looking at his watch. I was being paid by the hour, see, and he was timing me to find out if I was cheating him. Professors are like that—a little windblown in the attic."

Owen put down the napkin and turned the watch to the candlelight to read the inscription. It was necessary to squint to make out the fine lettering.

"*Jehoshaphat,* Kelly!"

The woman jumped at the sharp cry. "What is it?"

"You dug up Pastor Coulson!" He goggled at the woman.

"I do not know this . . . it."

"He, *him,* not it! I know him—he's from my hometown. Pastor Coulson's running around somewhere out there!"

"But that cannot be," she said reassuringly. "The males are not permitted outside after dark."

"Then he's in somebody's back room sleeping around!"

It boggled the mind. Pastor Coulson, the pillar of Hartford City, alive and well and sleeping in some dolly's back bedroom. Well—sort of alive, and ambulatory. The good pastor had been resurrected first and set to work somewhere; he had arrived in town before Owen and learned firsthand that his preachings were something less than accurate. It must have been a stunning blow. The man hadn't been seen during the day's wanderings, but that wasn't to be remarked. Owen had seen or had contact with only a fraction of the hundreds of workmen riding the road or toiling in the factories. Here, somewhere, was a man from the future, a man who had outlived Owen and gone on to nobody knew how many years into the future. Pastor Coulson might even know who had won the war in Europe.

"Kelly, you do the damndest things! You dig me up and dump me on the stoop next door, and now you've gone and dug up Pastor Coulson." He finished the last of his coffee and let the remaining whiskey roll down his throat. "This is a fine kettle of fish."

"What is a fish?"

Kehli had turned her chair about to watch Owen wash the dishes. The meal had been an impressive one, revealing his unsuspected skills in a day already full of surprises, and she was not slow in realizing that the man was more than a transitory variant. The fact that he was doing housekeeping chores without being ordered to do so was not lost on her. The city had never known a male quite like him before—at least, not in her thirty years of life.

His coming reformation would be a loss.

Owen had been obliged to go to the machine and whip up a dishpan and a box of Ivory Flakes because there were none in the house. He wrapped one bath towel about his middle to serve as an apron and used another as a dish towel. When the chore was finished and the dishes stacked away, he scooped up the booty and returned it to its box and then washed off the table.

"Mind if I keep the pocket watch? I don't guess Pastor Coulson can tell time anymore."

"You may have it, Owen Hall."

"Thanks. If I run across him and he wants it, I'll give it back, of course. Honest as the day is long, I am." He poked a finger through the treasure. "There ain't no money here—dimes and quarters and shuls and stuff. I saw some at Paoli's house."

"I give the coins to her. She wishes to collect them."

"Most women would want the jewelry—there's a fat bundle wrapped up in these stones." Owen picked up a string and dangled it before her eyes. "These look like real pearls to me—maybe several hundred dollars worth here. Some women would do some high diddling for these. Don't ask what that means. You lead a sheltered life."

"We do not wear jewelry. The artifacts were thought to be religious objects worshipped by the ancients."

Owen eyed the woman. "Out of the mouths of babes." He dropped the pearls into the box and gave the remaining loot another scrutiny. Some of the objects in the box were mildly surprising. Of what use were spectacles to a corpse? The undertaker might as well include a radio in the coffin.

"Whatever happened to the wristwatches? There's just got to be some wristwatches turning up now and then. I had one once, but somebody lifted it."

"What is a wristwatch?"

Owen said, "Fudge," and explained a watch, using his pocket timepiece for points of reference and comparison. He wrapped his fingers about his left wrist to show Kehli how and where he'd worn his.

"We *do* find those objects, Owen Hall. Like the coins, they are collected. Wytha has many of them."

"Is she one of your neighbors too?"

"Wytha lives a distance away, beyond the zone. She sits on the council of administrators."

"I knew it!" Owen declared with fervor. "I just *knew* it. Leave it to a politician to peel the boodle off a body." He smacked a hand onto the table. "I've got a notion to march right down there and get my watch back!"

Kehli looked over the table with quick alarm and reached out to stay his hand. "That would be very unwise, Owen Hall. An imprudent action would be cause for grave concern. Wytha has a fitful temper."

"Meaning she would throw me in the slammer?"

"I don't know what she would do, but it would be unpleasant for you." She enfolded his hand in hers. "And please do not make noise. People may be sleeping around us."

"I ought to pound on the wall and keep old what's-her-name awake all night." He jerked the thumb of his free hand at the separating wall behind him. "I owe her one.

"Please do not do that. Her name is Hoon."

"It's just a—oh, yes, Hoon. Good old Hoon, the woman with a thousand friends. What does she do, Kelly?"

"Do?"

"What's her job in this here town? I can't figure her messing around with bootleg booze."

"Hoon is the keeper of the records. An archivist."

"Archivist, anarchist—I don't care a moldy fig about her politics. Does she keep all kinds of records? Births, deaths, the guys you dig up—that kind of thing?"

Kehli nodded. "She maintains a record of all that occurs in the city—the vital statistics, the number of recoveries as well as the losses, the amount of foodstuffs produced and consumed, the rebuilding and repairs, the laws and regulations handed down by the council of administrators—oh, whatever is necessary to maintain a continuous record. We pride ourselves on our history and she is the city historian. The ancients did that."

"We've got town clerk and county clerks who do the same thing." Owen considered the matter. "What about a library, or the Queen Bee's history reaching back a long spell? Paoli told me something this afternoon. She said that she searched the files and found out about boozing in the old days. What files?"

"Hoon is the keeper of the files. There are many written records that you would call a library. They include our limited knowledge of the ancients, but there is much dispute as to whether the writings are truth or fantasy. Some are regarded as being only Mother's stories."

"King Tut is real but Buck Rogers is fantasy. There ain't nobody been walking on clouds lately." He squeezed her hand and grinned. "Guess what Hoon did?"

"I cannot guess."

"She found out that the workshop machines will do more than make zombies for the factories—just as you did an hour ago. She found out they would also make booze, and—by damn!—she did. Between you and me and the gatepost, Kelly, it was mighty poor stuff—it was dime-a-shot bar whiskey, pure rotgut, but she made some on her own machine and got tanked. Plastered. And while she was plastered she made a variant for herself. Me." Owen Hall paused and thought about that for a length of time. At last he said, "Ugh."

Kehli was cautious. "That may be true."

"She *was* drunk, I *am* here. I'm a variant."

"It appears to be true."

"How did she get a corpse? If she's the town clerk and keeper of the files, why is she cranking out retreads for slave labor? Doesn't she have enough work to keep busy? Why did you deliver *me* to her door yesterday?"

"It was so directed."

"Come again?"

"Her name and number was on the delivery list given to me. Each day I am given a quota to recover and a list of addresses where they are to be delivered. I do not question my directives, Owen Hall."

"Where do you get the lists?"

"The council decides on the number of recoveries, but my directives are issued by Hoon or the woman who is assisting her."

"Did you get yesterday's list from Hoon?"

"Yes." Kehli seemed suddenly uncomfortable.

Owen fell silent and rested his case. It was pleasant to be holding hands across the table with the woman, and he was more than willing to ignore the fact that she was two years the elder. What were a few years between good friends?

Watching her face by candlelight was an entrancing pastime, and the flames appeared to increase the depths of those marvelous brown eyes. He had fallen in love with her eyes first. She was a heady delight to look at, to be with, and he was ever so pleased that he'd found her in the timber. It was hurtful to realize that he would have to leave her behind; of all the people in the town, he would miss only *her*, and that absence would be keenly felt. Perhaps he could sneak back to the timber now and then and watch her at work, watch her napping or lunching on a pink blanket under the trees. Perhaps he could come back for periodic visits while he explored the prairies and sought out other towns, while he searched for Indiana.

He said to the heady delight, "I'd take you out for a night on the town, if there was any nightlife around here. What do you do for fun?"

"I sometimes sing."

"Sing—for fun? You mean sing like Bing Crosby and Al Jolson or sing like in the Tabernacle Choir? I heard the Tabernacle Choir on the radio once."

"I am not familiar with those . . . names."

"They're all ancient people, but some are more ancient than others. Who do you sing with?

"I sing alone, to please myself."

"I'd rather shoot pool," he replied.

"What is pool? Is it a body of water?"

"It's a game you play with balls on a table. Cupcake, there's an awful lot of things you don't know, even if you are a neato citizen of the future. You and Paoli are always asking what is this, what is that, and what is the other thing, and a guy would think that the schools are pretty poor around this town." Owen interlaced his fingers with hers and gently squeezed. "You failed to pick up on one little thing. You didn't ask me what love is."

Kehli looked at him for a length of time and then slowly smiled. "There was no need to ask."

"Ah," Owen murmured, and again: "Ah. . . ." He measured the warmth of her smile. "Are you in the mood to do anything about it? I'm a jitterbug expert."

"There is nothing I could do if I wished. It is forbidden."

"Has the council passed laws against that too?" He was thunderstruck. "Kelly, that's a crock!"

She made a little moue with her lips, cautioning him to keep his voice down. "The rule is as old as the city itself. A woman may not form an emotional attachment for a recovery. It is considered degrading and could lead to future problems. It is forbidden, Owen Hall."

"That's un-American. So what about the variants?"

"Variants are permissible because they perform a physical function only, and their duration is limited."

"How limited?" he asked with suspicion.

"They are usually kept one or two days."

"How do you like that!" Owen cried. "Dig 'em, diddle 'em, and dump 'em. It's enough to make a man take to drink!" He pulled his hands free and emptied the remainder of the bourbon into his coffee cup. If Kehli had not been seated across the table and had not asked him to keep the peace, he would have hurled the empty bottle at the wall of Hoon's bedroom. "What happens to the poor old variants after they're all used up?"

"They are remolded for the labor force."

"Heads _or_ tails, I lose." Owen was indignant; it just wasn't right to treat an Indiana gentleman in such a fashion. He fixed the woman with a steely gaze. "Do you feel degraded, Kelly?"

"I am not degraded by your company, Owen Hall. I seldom understand you and I think your ancient peoples were a mad lot, but you have provided an excellent meal, you have taught me much, and you are an entertaining visitor. I have liked you since we met this morning, and I feel strangely exhilarated while in your presence. No, I am not degraded."

"Well, bully for the good guys. Go ahead and sing if you feel like it, cupcake. It probably won't mean anything to you, but I _don't_ expect you to pay for your supper, no way, no how. If you want to sing, I'll hum along. Do you know "After the Ball Is Over?"

An imperious rapping sounded at the door.

"Geez," Owen muttered, "it's over already."

He sidled out of his chair as Kehli jumped, startled at the sound. Her expression was a mixture of alarm and dismay. She stared at him for a long, agonizing moment, as if she were mentally bidding him farewell, and went to the door.

Owen blew out the candles and sped away with the speed and dispatch of a timorous swain bolting through the back door even as an angry father came in the front. He left behind as evidence a measure of bourbon, a half-smoked cigar, and his two rucksacks.

Twelve

Though a man escape every other danger, he can never wholly escape those who do not want such a person as he is to exist.

—Demosthenes

Owen didn't stop running until he tripped and fell over a cross-pipe hidden in the weeds. He sprawled on the ground for a long moment, breathing through his mouth to regain his spent breath, and then cautiously raised his head to look back.

The fireflies had resumed their pointless dance.

He had put nearly a quarter-mile between him and the torch-bearing manhunters. It wasn't much and it surely wasn't a safe distance, but a quarter-mile was pretty good for a man fresh out of retirement. His legs and his lungs had gotten a mite rusty from disuse during the last several hundred years and weren't quite ready for emergencies. Owen thought he had a few minutes grace to catch his breath. The manhunters were wasting time by running along the backs of the row houses checking doors, believing he had entered yet another one, but they would get the smarts in short order and realize where he really was.

By now there were thirty or forty women in the posse, if the number of torches provided an accurate count; there could be double that number if others had come along empty-handed. He certainly was a popular fugitive.

Somebody had finked on him—somebody had overheard him talking with Kehli and called in the dogs of the law. A party pooper. That was the trouble with neighbors having thin walls—they always begrudged the people next door throwing a party; they always betrayed themselves as soreheads when they weren't invited to join an orgy. (Not that he would *want* Hoon at an orgy. Owen didn't even want to think about the steamy night spent with Hoon after she resurrected him. There are some things man was not meant to know.)

Owen reached out to find and feel the pipe that had thrown him and wondered briefly why it was there. The pipe wasn't connected to anything and it ran at cross-purposes to all the others, but it was there and it was probable that others like it were ahead of him.

He scanned the sky, seeking Jupiter, and found it near the zenith; a surprising amount of time had passed while he was in the kitchen romancing Kehli. As yet there was no moon, but if one should rise later he'd stand out like a rogue zombie. Owen got to his feet and hastily changed his clothes, keeping a wary eye on the distant torches. They'd be howling after him soon like Indians after a tenderfoot and the pink coveralls were an easy target; the dun-colored garment was the better one for flight. He bundled up Paoli's pinks and tucked them inside his waist, not wanting to leave them behind to mark his trail.

Owen started off through the tangled weeds but then changed his mind and climbed atop the larger pipe for the inward journey. It was easier than walking a Pennsy rail, a balancing act he'd often done in his childhood. Indiana was chock full of rails for walking or for practicing broad jumps, and every once in a blue moon a boy could, if he was very lucky, find an unused fusee along the tracks. Fusees were glorious treasures to save for Fourth of July night or for New Year's Eve.

He'd give a shiny buffalo nickel to know what happened to Indiana—if he had a buffalo nickel.

What happened to Hartford City and Kokomo and Indianapolis, to the Pennsylvania and the New York Central tracks, to the old highway that crossed the Pennsy tracks and robbed him of his twenty-ninth birthday, and to all the farms along that highway? What happened to his boardinghouse and to the lumberyard where he traded? To his Ford truck? What happened to Dusty's

Bar in Galveston, to Juanita's Grocery in Hartford City, to Texas Tommy's Steak House on the north side of Indianapolis, and to the windmill on Brickyard Road that had been wired to generate electricity? What happened to President Roosevelt and to his old buddy Churchill over there in England?

Gone. All dead and gone. Hartford City and all those places were gone with Babylon and Jericho. Owen Hall and Pastor Coulson and the workmen were the only ones left alive from the old days, but you couldn't say much for the pastor and the zombies.

Somebody had done an awful lot of tearing down and rebuilding in the last several hundred years—or maybe it was a thousand, considering those stars overhead in their strange positions. Somebody had really wrecked the country. Maybe the United States had lost the war, or maybe it had been bombed out like those cities and towns in England, or maybe the NorAmerFed had made a clean sweep. *This* town wasn't a new Hartford City built on the ruins of the old one—not *this* crazy round town with the rolling road. The cemetery was a useful landmark, a stable mark, but it was in the wrong direction from the town. Hartford City used to be off there somewhere, to the west.

The powerhouse was an enigma.

The pipe from Kehli's house had carried Owen near the center of the circle before it merged with an adjoining twin. Smaller pipes had joined with larger pipes and the larger pipes later merged with huge pipes as he approached the center, and in the end Owen was forced to abandon his pipe walking and descend to the ground. He worked a slow and tortuous path through the maze. The pipes had evolved into a plumber's nightmare, and every one of them ended at the powerhouse; they were welded into the walls of the giant structure—the wackiest Rube Goldberg invention Owen had ever encountered—but nowhere could he find a point of entry for man or woman. The powerhouse sprouted a wilderness of pipes and resembled a metallic octopus, but it lacked a door, a window, a rat hole. The building was sealed.

Owen clambered over pipes and slid under pipes, fighting weeds every foot of the way, circling the structure twice searching for a way in before admitting defeat.

Food and water came out of the powerhouse to serve the row houses but people didn't enter it to tend or tinker with the machinery. He had to admit that it was the nearest thing to perpetual motion he'd yet seen. Maybe it was a weird spaceship from Mars or Venus or one of those alien planets, come to earth to feed the natives; maybe the pink women had found it and taken advantage of it by hooking up their pipes for a lifetime of free handouts. But then again, maybe not. Owen eyed the looming bulk with speculation. Food also went *into* the thing—he could speak from experience about that.

Owen said, "Oh, fudge!" and rapped the metal wall in sudden recognition. It wasn't a spaceship from Mars.

He climbed up and through the maze and sat down astraddle the topmost pipe. The town was spread out around him in a near perfect circle, and he was looking down on the roof of the building just beyond his feet. No spaceship. Despite the dim light, he could now see all of the structure clearly, and he recognized it as the *very* big brother of the think-and-do machines in the factory, a giant-sized replica of the machine he had worked on. The design was the same, but the multitude of pipes had misled him, prevented him from knowing the machine at first sight. He had made bacon on one such machine during the morning, and *his* machine fed the bacon to *this* machine, where it would be dispatched to the row houses come morning. Kehli had ordered his overdone monkey wrench from here. The powerhouse was a transshipment center and it was no wonder he couldn't find a door into the thing; the pink ladies would be both surprised and displeased to find pieces of Owen mixed in with their eggs and bacon at breakfast. He would likely spoil their appetites.

Owen craned his neck to look behind him and found the dark line of buildings that he called downtown—the zone containing City Hall and the factories. He squinted in the darkness, struggling to separate roofline from skyline. The pipe he sat on appeared to lead into one of those buildings. He stood up carefully, found his balance, and advanced a dozen paces along the pipe before a flicker of firelight caught his eye.

Owen stopped and turned to look.

The posse was coming through the jungle; they had at last realized his escape route and now the pack of them were spread out in a surprisingly wide search pattern, beating the bushes and working along the pipes in pursuit. Their sweep was slow but thorough, and already they had reached that quarter-mile point where he'd tripped and fallen.

Owen measured the pipe before him and the roofline in the distance. He thought he could make it to the nearest building if he ran. He could climb to the rooftops and find refuge there before the posse arrived at the center. But then, he hadn't been behind the door when the brains were passed out. He wasn't about to run along a pipe twenty feet above the ground in darkness—not even to escape an avenging horde. Owen turned about and retraced the dozen paces to the powerhouse and jumped down onto its roof. The footing was firm but gently sloping.

He flopped on his belly in the middle of the roof and turned his head to watch the approach.

There were thirty-six torches by count. The torches were so widely separated that the torch bearers would have missed him if he had been concealed between any two of them, so there had to be other women without light working the darker spaces between. Owen guessed that somebody had called out the marines. The posse had to number between the thirty-six and maybe fifty, sixty, or seventy women. He couldn't con or sweet-talk that many. If *that* mob discovered him, he would be reconstituted pork before you could say Jack Armstrong.

Owen hugged the roof and waited.

The huntresses came on with grim purpose and soon the faces and the pink uniforms of those in between without fire could be seen in the torchlight. The weeds were trampled, the few bushes that might have offered concealment were beaten down, and the undersides of every large pipe was searched. A chipmunk would not have escaped discovery.

The maze slowed their march. It was more difficult to climb through a tangle of pipes and peer beneath each and every one as well, and the really large pipes near the center offered better hiding places. Owen was thankful he hadn't remained on the ground; they would have found him by now unless he had circled the powerhouse and run for the distant row houses on the opposite side.

Which is what the manhunters did, but not on the

run. They split into two groups when they reached the
powerhouse, searched about its base in the same method-
ical manner, and regrouped on the far side. The operation was stalled for several minutes when someone called
a war council. One woman wanted the posse split into
three groups so that they could fan out into the three remaining directions simultaneously, but she was voted
down. Another, a woman with a soft but confident tone
of voice, argued that the culprit would flee in a straight
line to the opposite side of the circle in search of unlocked doors, that the wisest course of action would be to
follow him there and *then* split into two groups, with each
group working back along the wall line until they met
again at the starting point. She was of the opinion that
when Owen found all the doors locked against him, he
could be herded ahead of them and trapped when the
two groups again came together. If, by chance, he managed to elude them in the darkness, he would surely be
found when another hundred women joined the manhunt
at sunrise. The plan was seconded and carried.

Owen turned his head on the rooftop to watch them
go, but then counted the torches a second time to make
certain they hadn't left one behind to snare him when he
came out of hiding. There would be no way of knowing
—until he moved—whether or not the sneaky devils had
left behind a shadow without a torch.

Owen stayed put until the posse was half a mile gone
and then crept away on big cat feet. He lifted himself
cautiously from the rooftop and scanned the pipe maze
below in search of a shadow, a flash of pink, an upturned
face. Walking softly and without sound, he crossed the
roof to the edge of the maze of ducts and mounted the
pipe he'd left only a short while before. There should be
a factory at the other end of it and a means of reaching
the road.

Again he stopped to scan the darkness below and then
to stare after the receding torches. He stood poised,
watching and listening, but there was no outcry. Jupiter
had moved another hour across the sky.

Owen marched off along the pipe with high confidence,
mindful of his height off the ground and maintaining his
balance by holding his arms outstretched and keeping his
gaze firmly fixed on the narrow path ahead of him. Even
in the night it was easier than walking a thin Pennsy rail

by daylight. Old Indiana railbirds never lost their touch.

Behind him on the ground, unseen and unheard, two tall shadows emerged from concealment to follow the pipe walker. The shadows were careful to keep their distance and not crowd their quarry, careful not to betray their presence; they were content to tag along at an easy pace, following the silhouette balanced against the sky.

A factory wall met his outstretched fingers.

Owen flattened himself against the wall and reached overhead to grope for the roofline. The building had no eaves and the roof edge was just above his head; he thought he could pull himself up and climb onto the roof easily enough, but first he wanted to investigate the ground below the pipes. The darkness underneath was complete, but there should be doors somewhere in the factory wall—doors opening out into the jungle. Owen clambered down the pipes and ran his fingers along the back wall in search of a latch, strap, or doorknob. An ill-fitting door was soon discovered, but it was locked against him. He braced one foot against the wall for leverage and pulled, but the door remained firm. He lacked a screwdriver in his pockets.

"Fudge!"

Owen worked his way through yet another tangle of pipes and continued the search of the back walls, finding two more doors that were locked. A man would think that the townspeople had panicked and locked everything against an army of rapacious burglars—or else the doors had been sealed for a century since the day the pipes were connected and the factories opened. The fire marshall should have something to say about that.

Owen gave up the search in disgust and climbed the nearest set of pipes to the rooftop, pulling himself over the edge and grunting at the exertion. He dropped on his belly to catch his breath, squirmed because of a lump pressing against the belly, and finally raised his head to look for the distant torches. The posse had reached the far side of town, and as he watched, the torchbearers split into two groups to follow opposing walls around the inside circle. The group on his side would be below him after a while. It was time to move on.

He rolled away from the edge and found that the roof had a very slight pitch from front to back; it was no more than two or three degrees, but it insured the runoff of rainwater. The roof was also alarmingly spongy under his weight, another indication of poor carpentry work—the joists were too far apart and the roofing material was as thin as a politician's pledge.

Owen got to his feet, gingerly tested the surface under him, and walked to the front roofline to peer into the blackness below. He thought he could see the ground, and if he really was seeing it, the grass and the rolling road were more than twenty feet below—much too far away to risk hanging by his hands and dropping. A pioneer setting off to explore a new world with a couple of broken legs had little chance of capturing a horse or bringing down a buffalo. He backed away from the edge and decided to circle the town by rooftop, turning first to the southwest, where the houses of Kehli and Paoli were.

A pioneer had urgent need of the supplies in those two rucksacks that had been left behind.

Owen put his hand and arm upright before his face and advanced slowly. He hadn't seen a radio anywhere in the town, but that wasn't proof they didn't exist somewhere, here or there, and radio antennas were *always* stretched across rooftops at the exact height of a man's neck. That seemed to be a perverse rule of thumb. The building he was walking on was higher than the nearby dwellings, so the roofline had to drop off somewhere. He proceeded with caution.

The beginning was easy.

The roof of the adjoining building was the same height as the one he stood on, but the structure next beyond was a few inches lower, while the bacon factory or gin mill after that one was again lower by an inch or so. Owen kept going with a singleness of purpose but at a slow and frustrating pace. Here a roofline jutted higher against the night sky, forcing a climb, but there the structure was lower and he descended once more in pursuit of his goal; sometimes only a small ridge separated two roofs, but at other times there was no line of demarcation at all and it was useless to attempt a count of the number of buildings traversed. Owen said to hell with it, he wasn't taking a census, and trudged on. When his left foot suddenly lost the spongy surface and dangled in empty space, he backed off and lay down on his stomach to reconnoiter. He rested on a lump.

He reached over the side of the building and waved a hand to and fro in the night air. Nothing below him obstructed the free passage of his hand. The roofing material was black and no solid surface met his questing gaze, but he thought he had come to the end of the zone and reached the first of the dwellings where the good citizens should be sleeping—if they all weren't running around carrying torches and hunting a fugitive.

"So now what, Horace Greeley?"

Owen rested and puzzled the blackness below. When he realized that the lump against his stomach was the pilfered pink coveralls he pulled them out with a sound of self-derision and shook them out to their full length. The coveralls were held by the neck and dangled over the edge to the very limit of his reach. The bottoms of the trouser legs created a soft swooshing sound on the rooftop below as he dragged the garment to and fro.

"Jackpot, Mr. Greeley."

Owen tied the coveralls about his waist, lowered himself carefully over the roof edge, and dropped. The new rooftop cracked under his falling weight with a sound that resembled a small-bore cannon fired into a stilly night.

"*Geez,* do they ever need a carpenter around this town. If I wanted to hang around, I'd apply for the job."

Owen pulled his feet out of the hole in the roof.

He still had a respectable distance to travel and no guideposts to lead him to the correct house. The timber and the cemetery first glimpsed in the early morning were now hopelessly lost in the darkness, and looking out across the pipe jungle to the moving torches was of no help; those eager manhunters could be anywhere along the inside rim of the circle. The only reliable indication of his goal would be at or near the point where the two parties came together again, and he would have to seek out the specific house from there, sneaking inside one after another, if need be, in search of those precious rucksacks.

Owen put the protective arm before his face and struck off into the southwest at a quickened pace. He was quickly thankful for the absence of chimneys and vents. The roofs beneath him sagged at his every footfall, while the creaks and groans of the timbers were enough to wake the sleepers in the bedrooms below. He glanced over his shoulder once at the torchbearers, found them surprisingly near, and edged closer to the front rooflines to put more distance between him and the manhunters. A bright moon would have betrayed him at once.

It was a patch-poor way for a law-abiding Indiana boy to spend the night. If he had his 'druthers, he'd 'druther be in a warm snug bed with Paoli or Kehli, doing what he had been resurrected to do. Kehli was his first choice.

Twin detonations crackled quickly behind him—two sharp crashes that resembled the sounds of small-bore cannons fired at his back. Owen whirled around but could not see his pursuers against the dark factory wall; they would need only a moment to pull their feet free of their holes and take after him. In the greater distance a torch flared above the zone rooftops, and as he watched another joined it—the troops were climbing the pipes and carrying the chase to higher elevations. There'd be precious little sleep tonight for the innocent citizens below.

Owen bounded away.

He was running perilously near the front roofline and was acutely aware that it continuously curved. For safety's sake he changed to the middle course, running along the centers and abandoning any hope of secrecy. The surface below his pounding feet sagged and creaked, behaving and sounding like a trampoline trainer. He stumbled over an unexpected ridge, caught his balance, and raced on. A querulous cry was raised from some apartment underfoot.

The noise made by his pursuers was shockingly close. Owen thought there were two of them and thought they were running at speed, unmindful of radio antennas or other obstacles. He dropped his protective arm and attempted to increase his own speed. The roofing protested.

Another treacherous ridge felled him.

He was forced into an ungainly dance in his effort to remain upright, hopping forward under his own pell-mell momentum. The dance faltered. One foot came down heavily and plunged through the top surface. Owen hastily yanked his foot out of the hole, hopped again, lost his balance, and toppled backward out of control. The poor sheathing cracked and splintered under his weight as his posterior drilled a new hole through the roof and then on through the fragile ceiling below it. Ignominiously, tail first, Owen plummeted downward onto a lady's bed. A solitary candle lit the bedroom.

The lady was in her shower.

She bolted out of the cubicle and gaped at the unexpected visitor. Her mouth was opened to screech.

Owen scrambled off the bed and rubbed his bruised backsides. He found time to appreciate the glistening wet body and thought the candlelight nicely complimented it.

"Hi, cutie. Want someone to wash your back?"

The lady stared at her holed ceiling and at the shattered roof. Debris littered the bed.

"Idiot male!"

"So's your old man."

The lady delivered the tardy screech and made a threatening gesture with two balled fists.

"I will *do* you."

"You've got it all wrong," Owen retorted. "You're supposed to say. 'Ho, varlet! Have at thee!' They do it in all the Errol Flynn movies."

The lady thrust forward in anger and grabbed at him, but a sudden racket on the rooftops stopped her advance in mid-stride. She stared upward with astonishment as the racket grew into an oncoming thunder. New debris fell.

"Make way for the varlets!" her visitor cried, and leaped clear of the target area. He eyed the ceiling.

Sandaled feet appeared in the ragged opening and in the next moment two hurtling bodies filled the hole, forcefully enlarging it as they fell through amid a shambles of timber and roofing material. Owen's pursuers crashed down together on the bed in a confusion of arms and legs, a mishmash of kicking feet and strangled cries. The bed collapsed under the impact. Someone pounded on the adjoining wall. An outraged hostess voiced her opinion of the invaders and their uncouth method of entry.

Owen turned to flee, but then hesitated only long enough to offer neighborly advice.

"Cutie, you'd better put something on and get ready for company. There's a whole damn' army right behind them!"

He ran through the house to the front door and yanked it open, then just as quickly leaped backward from the doorway. Two wardens stood just down the way, staring dumbstruck at the place on the rooftop where their sisters had been only moments before. Owen turned desperately in the darkness, seeking refuge, and then crawled into the only concealment available to him:

the cramped space beneath the workbench. His feet struck some solid object.

Quick exploration revealed a casket—a lightweight and streamlined casket identical to those encountered in the cemetery that morning. It was empty. Without second thoughts, Owen slithered into the coffin and attempted to pull the lid down over himself. The lid refused to fit well, a covering as poorly contrived as some of the doors to the houses. He held himself still to avoid discovery, struggling to control his breathing and meanwhile bemoaning his luck at selecting a factory reject.

The commotion in the bedroom seemed to be sorting itself out. The lady of the house had not stopped her angry complaints, but one of the intruders was trying to placate her, while the other was attempting to explain why they were on the roof in the first place. Neither attempt at pacification was wholly successful, but the volume of sound diminished. Someone—one of the wardens—called through the open doorway. The three women in the bedroom responded on the run and there was a headlong rush past the casket and out into the night to search for the fugitive who had only narrowly escaped their clutches.

The lady of the house rushed right back in again when she remembered her nudity.

Owen kept his place and waited silently, listening to the sounds of the woman dressing. When her sandals passed him and the door was closed from the outside, he slipped back the coffin lid and raised his eyes above the rim to reconnoiter. The candle still burned in the bedroom, but nothing moved in its dim glow. The workshop appeared to be equally empty. He crept out of the coffin and rested on his knees beside the workbench for a moment, testing the air. The house was silent.

Owen padded softly to the back door and slid the bolt. He applied one eye to a slim crack in the door and scanned the weedy jungle. A number of women were still beating the bushes on the opposite side of the circle, working their appointed way around to the meeting place at Kehli's or Paoli's house. Owen marveled that they had missed—or ignored—the circus on the rooftops. He closed the door without a sound but left it unlocked. The next object to fall under his scrutiny was the workman lying on the bare cot in the back room.

Owen hesitated beside the cot, eyeing the man.

"Barney, I could use you, but it would be a damned dirty trick to play on you." Owen contemplated the man's usefulness but then shook his head. "Can't do it, Barney."

The zombie failed to express his appreciation.

Owen returned to the entrance and cautiously peeked outside, poised to run again if need be. The area immediately in front of the house was unpopulated. He opened the door wider and put his head around the doorframe to scan the nearby lawns and the rolling road. The nearest women were a distance away, while those bearing torches were yet farther down the road. Owen eased through the door, closed it softly behind him, and shot down the narrow sidewalk and across the road to leap into the high grasses that promised concealment. There was no outcry. He waited a moment to make certain that he hadn't been seen and then worked his slow way deeper into the grasslands, wanting to put a greater distance between himself and that road and the city it served. The road builders had never thought to maintain a mowed shoulder on the far side.

Only the vital backpacks waiting at Kehli's house kept him from bolting for the timber and the open prairie. Those packs were as necessary as Texas Tommy's treasury.

He continued his determined journey into the southwest, seeking the proper house. Bands of women roved the road searching for the missing culprit—determined manhunters who knocked on doors, opened doors, swept through empty apartments, scanned the rooftops, peered into the high grasses just off the road, and endlessly asked one another futile questions.

His old nemesis Hoon provided the verbal guidepost that led Owen home—she of the muscular build and the booming voice. Owen popped up in the grass to seek the source of the voice and found Hoon standing just outside an open doorway, her great hands balled on her hips. Hoon was haranguing two monitors who had just completed their search of the nearby empty apartment, monitors who appeared to be already short of temper and unappreciative of Hoon's noisy encouragements. The women mounted the rolling road and broke into a trot, the sooner to put a distance between themselves and the behemoth.

Owen watched and waited.

When the night grew quiet again and no other wardens happened along to become victims of verbal abuse, Hoon turned and entered the doorway. The door stayed open but Owen couldn't remember if that door was one he'd borrowed or not. The interior of the house was not illuminated. He eyed the dark opening with suspicion. A thousand little old ladies of both sexes in Indiana made a habit of sitting behind their screen doors or behind their windows, watching every living thing that passed: man, woman, child, or dog.

Owen turned and retraced his path, moving away from Hoon's house. When he had gone a reasonable distance he left the concealing grasses, crossed the road on the run, and flattened himself against the nearest house wall.

No one raised a cry of discovery.

Owen inched his way along the walls toward Kehli's dwelling, taking care to tiptoe past every door and not make noise crossing the narrow sidewalks. Darkness enveloped his stealthy advance and he counted the doors to measure his advance. Hoon's place was near.

He stopped at Kehli's doorway, softly tested the latch and found it unlocked, then eased the door open. The apartment was in darkness.

A heavy hand thwacked him across the back while an equally heavy foot slammed into his shins, simultaneously knocking him forward and tripping him. Owen fell headfirst toward the door, rebounded off it, and went down gasping for breath. His mouth was filled with growing grass. The woman who had felled him pinioned his legs and bellowed her triumph.

"Caught you, dummy!"

Owen raised his head to spit out the mouthful of grass. He tried to turn his head to look at Hoon, but she slapped him alongside the ears in a stinging blow. He managed only a single word before she pushed his face into the ground.

"Cossack!"

Thirteen

Reason is the life of the law; nay, the common law itself is nothing else but reason. . . . The law, which is perfection of reason.

—Sir Edward Coke

City Hall wasn't worthy of the name.

It had been, and perhaps still was, a large warehouse or peanut butter factory with a cleared space in the middle that permitted the citizens to assemble for the redress of their grievances or to play bingo. Four of the very large resurrection machines were placed along one wall, while a stack of fifty or sixty spanking new coffins were neatly arranged along the opposite wall. In between were a half-dozen rigid, uncomfortable chairs for visiting citizens, a table just long enough to seat three councilwomen without too much crowding, and a smaller table behind the large one to accommodate the keeper of the records.

Owen Hall took a dim view of the courtroom and its inhabitants.

He held an even dimmer view of the woman seated at the small table, a woman who held a pen poised over an open record book. Hoon kept her face carefully expressionless except for those moments when she happened to catch Owen's eye, and then the expression was one of malicious triumph. It was a poor way to regard the man who had probably given her the experience of her life, even involuntarily.

The three councilwomen were markedly less inspiring.

Owen recognized with dismay the frowning elderly woman sitting in the center position behind the table: she had to be Wytha, who collected wristwatches off the bodies that were brought in from the excavations—Wytha, who had bossed the bacon factory where Owen worked briefly the previous day. Everything about Wytha but the uniform was monotonously gray: hair, eyes, skin, temper. The gray granny gave the impression of being newly roused from her sleep and none too happy about it; her face was as sour as pig swill. The factory whistle was absent from her neck.

The two remaining judges were strangers to Owen— at least, he didn't remember seeing them in his journeys about the city. The one sitting at the left end of the table was openly curious and inquisitive, a middle-aged woman who studied the prisoner with an admixture of voyeurism and distaste. Owen thought she had beady little eyes. The third judge, the younger woman seated at the right end of the table, was self-composed and bland—deceptively bland. Owen distrusted the woman on first sight.

All in all, three towering pillars of justice.

"They'd lynch me to watch the dance," he muttered.

"*Hush,*" Kehli whispered.

Kehli, a benumbed Paoli, and a warden sat on three of the six chairs in the center of the hall a short distance from the council table. Kehli was distressed and uncomfortable, although she strove to conceal that unhappy state and give the appearance of attentive neutrality. The little deceit was transparent—she fidgeted too much. Paoli was stiffly upright, glum, and still suffering the hangover. She kept her gaze fixed on the councilwomen and refused to acknowledge Owen's presence. The third person sitting in the row of chairs—the nameless warden—had to be a witness for the prosecution, because she held three neatly wrapped packages in her lap as she waited for the proceedings to open. Owen looked down over her shoulder to see a necktie, a ball pen hammer, and a cucumber.

He stood behind the chairs, his hands bound in front of him and a hefty warden clutching his arm to prevent an escape. The warden's clutch was none too gentle. All the doors of City Hall were closed and guarded.

Wytha signaled Hoon, and Hoon began to read.

"The male standing before the council is identified as Reclaimant. Two-six-oh-seven-oh-two, estimated age at about thirty. The male was found on the road at the proper hour yestermorning en route to the zone, but was obviously disoriented and unsure of his purpose. When found, the male was on his hands and knees examining the road itself.

"Paoli, Three-five-oh-three-five-oh, questioned him and determined that he was seriously flawed. The male could not identify his originating patron or his assigned place of shelter; he was unsure of his reason for being on the road and vague about his instructions for the day's work; he did not know or could not remember a place of shelter for the coming night. His speech was incoherent and his behavior was abnormal. Paoli gave him instructions for reporting to work and then for reporting to her shelter at the end of the day. She had determined that the male should be reconstituted in the proper manner and would thereafter be of useful service to the city.

"The male appeared for work at the food-processing center managed by Wytha, Two-one-oh-three-seven, although he had not been specifically assigned to that task. Wytha recognized the disorientation and abnormality and, after establishing his identification and newly assigned place of shelter, gave him instructions in the preparation of foodstuffs. The male performed his duties well while under Wytha's supervision but deviated from his instructions and reverted to abnormal behavior when Wytha went about her duties elsewhere. In his abnormal state the male produced a hammer, an unknown object fashioned from cloth, and a poison fruit—all of which he committed to the distribution center. The three foreign objects are waiting before the council."

"That's a barrel of buffalo chips! A cucumber ain't no poison fruit—it's a vegetable you eat, dummy."

The warden clutching the prisoner pinched his arm to silence him. The third judge—she of the bland countenance sitting on the right end—dropped her vanilla mask and stared at Owen with amazement. The room was dramatically silent.

Right End asked, "The male has the power of independent speech?"

"Damn right I do," Owen shot back. "It's one of the President's four freedoms and I make good use of it."

"Where did you obtain the use of independent speech?"

"From my maker, bless her fat hide." Owen thought it was high time to get in a few good licks of his own.

"Who was your originator? Do you remember?"

"Of course I do. I'll *never* forget Sweetiepie." He raised both hands to point a finger. "Good old Hoon made me what I am today. She wanted something special, see?" The sneaky devil had tried to cover her own involvement.

Right End swiveled her head to stare with surprise at good old Hoon and then turned back to the prisoner. Hoon's face was flushed and she kept her head down over the books. Wytha had never left off her cold gray appraisal of the culprit. Left End—she of the beady eyes —inspected the male with a new interest and waited for the next question. The mind behind the beady eyes had already guessed the answer.

Right End asked the next question. "What do you mean by special? Was there a special usage?"

"Yep. I'm a variant, and a damned good one, cutie. Good old Hoon whipped up a batch last night."

He felt a curious wriggling motion in the clutch on his arm and slanted his eyes to that side. His captor was silently giggling and shaking with the giggle. The judge seated at the right end had again turned to look at Hoon.

Wytha spoke through stiff gray lips. "*Amend* the record to present an accurate account of the male's origin and first place of shelter."

Hoon dipped her head in acknowledgment. "It will be done."

"Continue," Wytha ordered.

Hoon read: "When it was learned that a number of foreign objects had been committed to the distribution center, Wytha stopped work and sent the males employed there back to their shelters. The exact number of foreign objects produced by the abnormal male has not been determined, but a search has revealed several tools, many pieces of cloth similar to the one before the council, and a box of strange design that has no known purpose. The search for other foreign objects is continuing and it is realized that an unknown number of meals will be lost."

"Wait till they find the buzz saw," Owen muttered.

Kehli squirmed on the chair and whispered, "Hush."

"It has been determined that the male did not return to his shelter as directed but instead went outside to the excavations and engaged Kehli, Three-four-seven-six-one-six, in conversation. Kehli was not aware of events in the city caused by the male's behavior, but learned by questioning that he had been assigned to Paoli's shelter. She kept the male with her excavation crew until the day's task was completed and then returned him to the city. It is believed that the male then went directly to Paoli's shelter and destroyed the door to gain entrance. At a later hour, when Paoli discovered the missing door and protested his behavior, the male removed several nearby doors. One was used to replace the broken door the others were discarded.

"The male before the council caused other males to carry some doors to their shelters on the pretext that they had won them in a gambling game. It is not believed that the abnormal male taught the others to gamble."

"This town is ripe for bingo," Owen observed.

"How did this male cause that to happen?" Right End asked curiously. "Why did the other males follow his directions or instructions?"

Hoon said, "He was wearing stolen clothing."

The warden clutching Owen raised her free hand to display the wrinkled pink coveralls that had been removed from around his waist. The judges studied the garment.

"Where did he obtain the clothing?"

City Hall was silent. Those witnesses present either didn't know or were unwilling to further involve themselves. Owen grinned at the silence and winked at the judge sitting on the right end. He let his gaze drift ever so casually toward Hoon behind the small table and then back to the curious councilwoman. It was an innocent ploy, of course, and no one had asked *him* a direct question; besides, it would be unsportsmanlike to make more trouble for the blonde dolly—she was having enough miseries with her hangover.

Wytha signaled again and the reading of the indictment went on.

"During the course of the day the male standing before the council caused Paoli, by misdirection or deceit, to swallow a poisonous liquid which made her both mentally and physically ill. A sample of the liquid is present on the council table, along with a partially consumed artifact called a cigar."

Owen knew the inevitable question was coming and waited for Right End to ask it. She was looking at him.

"Where did the male obtain the poisonous liquid?"

"From the same place where Hoon got hers, judge. Right out of the resurrection machines you got here."

Right End swiveled her head once more to stare at the recorder. "Is that a true answer?"

Hoon admitted that it was. Her teeth were so tightly clenched that her tongue had difficulty maneuvering between them to make the reply.

"It ain't all that poisonous, judge," Owen advised Right End. "Take a little nip and see for yourself—or better yet, let me demonstrate."

Wytha motioned Hoon to continue the reading.

"At one point during the afternoon, Paoli and the male were observed together unclothed on the lawn before Paoli's shelter. Both were wet. The male dried Paoli's body and then followed her inside after speaking lasciviously to two persons who chanced upon the scene. Paoli and the male were not seen again for several hours."

"I was giving her a suntan," Owen explained. "All us old ancient peoples did it."

"Paoli suffered a severe illness from the poisonous liquid and went to bed, where she slept for several hours. When she awoke, the male had left the shelter and entered the forbidden area behind the shelters."

Owen looked down over Paoli's drooping shoulder. "It's nice to know you don't kiss and tell, lollypop." His captor yanked on his arm to silence him.

Left End councilwoman was studying him with a faintly lascivious expression—one that suggested she was reading between the historian's lines. Owen gave her the bold eye.

"The male concealed himself in the forbidden area and eluded the search parties who were entering all the shelters in that vicinity. It is not yet known how much injury the male caused to the conduits in the forbidden area. A survey to ascertain the extent of damage will begin at daylight. When the aberrant male wasn't immediately discovered and the search parties moved elsewhere, he came out of hiding and sought admittance to Kehli's shelter. Kehli detained him for a period of time until the shepherds could be summoned. During that time, the male drank the poisonous liquid and partially consumed the cigar now on the council table. Both gave off disagreeable odors suggestive of their toxic nature. The recorder, occupying the shelter next door, was awakened by the male's loud voice and boisterous behavior and immediately called the shepherds."

"Fink."

"The male again made his escape into the forbidden area, but this time the sheperds pursued him and prevented him from finding concealment there. By walking and jumping on the conduits, the fleeing male advanced to the center of the forbidden area and climbed atop the distribution unit, where he remained unseen until after the search party had passed. From the distribution unit the male proceeded to a building in the production zone and attempted to gain entrance. When that was denied him he climbed to the rooftops and ran along the roofs until he was trapped. Two shepherds discovered him on the rooftops and quickly followed him."

"Trapped? The rotten roof caved in."

"A considerable amount of damage was caused on and to the rooftops, but the full extent of the damage would not be known until daylight. When directly above the shelter of Tola, Three-five-one-oh-oh-nine, the male broke through the roof and jumped down onto the bed in a desperate attempt to evade his pursuers. He made lascivious suggestions to Tola, who attempted to capture him. The two shepherds following him descended into the shelter and continued their pursuit, aided by Tola. The truant male again made his escape through trickery and concealed himself in the darkness of the shelters, or perhaps along the road. A new search was organized.

"The male was finally captured by an alert recorder who reasoned and believed that he would eventually return to those patrons and shelters most familiar to him. The recorder waited patiently in the darkness and, as ex-

pected, discovered and subjugated the male as he was
again attempting to enter Kehli's shelter by stealth.

"The agent of uproar was promptly delivered into
the care of the shepherds and now stands before this
council for study and penalty. End of report."

"Well, hooray," Owen retorted. "Don't break your
arm while you pat yourself on the back." He faced the
table. "When do I get my say?"

"Males have no right to speak before this council,"
Wytha told him coldly. "Males are servants of the city."

"I protest! You might as well know, your honors, that
I'm going to appeal this to the circuit court. That testimony was loaded. Geez, you should *see* all the stuff that
was left out."

Without turning to look behind, Wytha asked, "Hoon,
is the *amended* statement a true and accurate one, without omissions?"

"Yes, Wytha."

"Paoli, is the amended statement a true and accurate
one, without omissions, to the best of your knowledge?"

Paoli glanced up from her protracted study of the
floor. She tried to sit up straight and appear attentive,
but the effort was just beyond her capabilities.

"Yes, Wytha."

"Kehli, is the amended statement a true and accurate
one, without omissions, to the best of your knowledge?"

Kehli stood up. "I did not know about the activities on
the rooftops, Wytha, but I would add information."

"Don't dig your own grave," Owen warned in a whis-
per. "Forget the chocolate cake!"

"What additional information is to be entered?"

Kehli said, "I talked to the male at some length before the shepherds arrived and he ran away in fear. He
responded readily to my questions and gave as much information as he was able to, but at no time did he offer
harm to me or to my shelter. This male is confused about
his death, which happened several hundred years ago,
and is even more confused about his reappearance here
in the city. He constantly seeks to learn the closure or
doom of his own native city and of the larger government to which his city paid allegiance. He bemoans the
loss of those who were his contemporaries and thinks
that some of them may now be serving our city because
they were interred in the same burial ground. An artifact

seen in my shelter once belonged to his companion and he recognized it as such. He was greatly distraught. At a future time, if the council agrees, I would like to include in our archives a summary of his background and his history as I understand it.

"It is apparent to me, and the council may agree, that the behavior of this male is the result of defective reconstruction, not a willful or malicious disregard for the city's customs and regulations. I do not criticize the faulty operation or the operator but do ask that the council consider his deficiency and his fearful state of mind as the real causes of his behavior. If it pleases the council, I am willing to become his patron and give him shelter."

Owen felt like shouting and applauding but knew better than to break the spell, if Kehli had been successful in casting a spell before the judges. She was the only friend he had in court, bless her delightful brown eyes, and he needed all the help he could find in this room. He'd be delighted to take shelter with her.

The councilwoman on the left end broke the spell.

She asked Kehli, "Is there a need for you to undergo a pregnancy examination?"

Kehli gasped with shock and turned red. "There is not!"

"That's rotten low-down dirty pool," Owen declared.

Left End turned her attention to Paoli. "Is there a need for you to undergo a pregnancy examination?"

The suffering blonde winced, stiffened in the chair, and then slumped once more. She mumbled, "I was ill from the poisoned drink." The hangover was monumental.

"Please speak up," Beady Eye persisted. "Is there a need?"

"I don't know," Paoli complained. "I don't *know.*"

Owen was thunderstruck. He looked down at Paoli and thought her either a magnificent liar who could become an accomplished actress, or else she had the worst memory of any woman he'd ever known—past life or this one.

City Hall was hushed with anticipation.

When Owen became aware of the prolonged silence and lifted his gaze to the council table he found the three pink-clad judges studying *him* with an eager intensity, awaiting his comment or testimony on the delicate matter at hand. Wytha had put aside her mask of cold dislike and for once seemed to invite his participation. The guards at the doors waited on his word. Hoon stared at him with a greedy desire to know, while Kehli and Paoli found safety in a dull examination of the floor.

Owen Hall tried to fold his arms but could not because his wrists were tied. He rested the palms of his hands on the chair in front of him and smiled sweetly at the three magistrates.

"We males have no right to speak before the council, ladies. We just run around serving the city."

Somebody sighed noisily. He didn't know if it was Paoli sighing with resignation or Hoon with frustration.

The three judges emerged from a huddle. Their heads had been together for long minutes.

Wytha stared at Owen and said sternly, "Hoon and Paoli will submit themselves to a pregnancy examination at the proper time. If, later, it has been determined that pregnancy has occurred, the fetuses will be put down. We are agreed that the possible birth of a male child is an unwanted event.

"As of now, the conversion and use of males for personal amusement and recreation is prohibited until an in-depth study of the practice is made. That study is hereby ordered. At a later date this council will rule on the question of again permitting variants for personal use or of permanently prohibiting them. The present example underscores the necessity of reexamining the whole question and, if they are again permitted, formulations of rules and responsibilities for their existence. Hoon is specifically reprimanded for her lack of responsibility."

"Demon rum was her downfall," Owen said. "Drink is the curse of the upper class."

"We must now assess the damage to the city. One door has been demolished and—"

"Two," Owen interrupted her.

"Two?"

"Good old Hoon smashed another one while she was chasing me. She's a clumsy lout."

Wytha favored him with the sour glare. "Two doors have been demolished and an unknown number of ruptures have damaged the rooftops. We must await a report on the condition of the conduits and of the various shelters that the male impermissibly entered and abused. Responsibility for his conduct and the subsequent damages will be allocated among Hoon, Paoli, Kehli, and myself. I include myself because of the male's aberrant conduct at the food center and the loss of future meals. Furthermore, the—"

"Oh, knock it off, Granny," Owen again interrupted. "You're crying over spilt milk. Now, I'm a carpenter and a good one—I guess I'm one of the best carpenters in my part of Indiana, all modesty aside. I can repair *all* that damage in no time, no time at all. Try me."

Right End asked curiously, "What is a carpenter?"

"Geez, honey, you're a— A carpenter is a skilled man who works with wood, who builds and repairs *anything* made of wood. I can build houses and porches, lay roofs, hang doors and windows and kitchen cabinets, lay floors—you name it, I can do it and do it *right*." Owen warmed up to his spiel. "Your honors, to be frank about it, you've got a rum town here. It's put together with chewing gum and kite string. The houses are skid-row tenements, the doors are sloppily cut and poorly hung, the rooftops are as thin as single-weight glass, and you don't seem to know what windows are. It's poor horse, all of it—it's amateur night at the Bijou—and all because you use those zombie workmen with no brains.

"I can change all that. I can start work bright and early tomorrow morning rebuilding the town like it *should* be built. You need to get those roofs fixed before the snows come. First thing to do is rip off that flimsy sheathing and use it for firewood or toothpicks and then set in more joists—all the joists should be sixteen inches on center for added strength, see? *Then* you can lay down heavy plywood sheathing and *then* cover it all with waterproof roofing. The sinks and the bathrooms need vents but all of it, everything, can be made in those resurrection machines over there.

"Ladies, when I'm done rebuilding this town it will bear up under a snow like we had in the winter of '88." He held his hands to his chest to demonstrate distance. "Why, do you know, back in Indiana I've seen snow belly-deep to a tall horse and you want to be *prepared* for that. What do you say, is it a deal?"

Left End asked curiously, "What is a snow?"

"There goes a good job." Owen sighed.

Right End offered a tart comment. "The males of the city are capable of that work."

"Oh, fudge! Ain't I getting through to you at all? Ain't you listening to me? The males of the city can't do anything *right* because you won't let them have brains—you won't let them think for themselves. I just told you—your shelters are flimsy, your doors don't fit, your roofs are cardboard, and your food is as thin as the stuff they give to poor people on welfare. There's a guy down there at the bacon factory who can't tell the difference between axle grease and shinola, but you've got him making butter."

Kehli whispered, "Owen Hall, *please . . .*"

The councilwomen stared at him in stony silence.

"What's more," Owen added, "you *eat* the gunk and think it's butter. Now that's dumb. All you've got to do is find a farmer or a dairyman, give him his brains, and set him to work. You'll soon have real butter and you'll kick yourselves for wasting all these years. The same goes for every other tradesman: carpenters, plumbers, roofers, electricians, shoemakers, the lot. Knock off this slavery business. Give men their brains and watch the changes get made. Let those zombies *think* and you'll see a whole new town around here. With electric lights maybe."

The hard silence continued.

"Take your time, think it over," Owen added with a wave of his hands. "This here town could be first class."

The councilwomen put their heads together to exchange glances and three words. Owen watched their lips and saw each pair of lips utter a single word.

Wytha said coldly, "We are agreed on the questions of atonement and reparations. Hoon will forfeit one meal a day for a total of twelve days. In addition, she will begin at once to rebuild and replace the damaged and dislocated doors to all the affected shelters. She will report back to this council when that task is completed. In the meanwhile she will relinquish her recording duties at the end of this session and turn those duties over to her assistant."

Hoon made no answer but nodded in acknowledgment and then favored Owen with a bitterly sour glance.

Wytha continued, "Paoli will forfeit one meal a day for a total of twelve days. In addition, she will begin at once to repair and rebuild the damaged rooftops and all

damaged shelters. She will report back to this council
when those tasks are completed. She is relieved of her
normal duties as a shepherd during the period of rebuilding."

Paoli mumbled, "It will be done." She eyed the floor.

Wytha stared hard at Owen. "I will forfeit one meal
a day for a total of twelve days for my laxity at the food
center. In the meanwhile I will begin a search for better
qualified males to process food and will report back to
this council when that is accomplished."

"It's about time," Owen commented.

Wytha said, "Kehli."

Kehli rose from her chair. Her face was pale.

"You are instructed to take this male to your shelter
under the guard of the shepherd. Additional shepherds
are to be placed at the doors of the shelter to prevent
another escape attempt. You will reconstruct the male in
the proper manner, conforming to all regulations concerning males in the service of the city. Specifically, you
are hereby instructed to remove his properties of independent thought, independent speech, and his abilities
as a variant.

"At the usual hour this morning you will bring him to
me for inspection. If the male has been satisfactorily re-
structured and if he is found to be fit and suitable for
labor, he will be assigned to a place of work and to your
shelter for safekeeping."

"I object!" Owen cried loudly. "I'm appealing this sentence to the Supreme Court."

Kehli said with distress, *"Please hush."*

"I won't hush. I'm not going to stand here like a dummy
and let them vote away my brains and my . . . uh, my
crown jewels. I demand to be heard by the Supreme
Court!"

Right End asked dryly, "What is a supreme court?"

"It's the place where you take your appeal when you
get a raw deal from the ribbon clerks. You're trying to
give me the short end of the stick here, but I refuse to
take it. I won't stand still for it. I demand an appeal.
Every citizen in Indiana has the right to appeal."

"There is no appeal from the decisions of this council,"
Wytha declared.

"I'm going to change that right now, Granny. You've
got a Supreme Court, whether you call it that or not, and

I want my case heard there before you start tinkering with anything! I want to present *my* side. I want to show the court how useful I am. Let's take it to the top."

Wytha stared at him in puzzlement. "I do not know what you are babbling about."

"Who's the real boss of this city?" Owen asked her. "Who's the top boss of all the cities, all thirty of them or however many you've got? Who has the last word? The Queen Bee, that's who—she's the Supreme Court."

Kehli cried out a warning. "Owen Hall!"

"What is a queen bee?" Wytha and Right End asked in unison. They were equally puzzled.

"Why, the Mother, that's who. The number one Mother, who sits on the throne and owns all these here towns. *She's* the Supreme Court around here, and I'm appealing to her. Now then, how can I find her? When can I set up a hearing? We're going to have justice in the good old American way. Where's Big Mother?"

City Hall was blanketed in stunned silence.

The guards at the doors were rigid and staring with shock. Hoon goggled. The tall shepherd holding him stiffened to attention and jerked his arm in brutal fashion. Despite her hangover, Paoli turned in her chair to look up at Owen with a startled expression that said he had committed a sacrilege. The judges were on their feet.

"What did I say?"

Owen watched without understanding while the three councilwomen thrust their heads together for yet another conference. Their faces were masks of cold fury. The heavy silence in the hall was venomous.

At last Wytha said, "Kehli!" Her voice was sharp.

Kehli waited, not trusting herself to speak.

"Previous instructions concerning the rehabilitation of this male are hereby canceled. We are now agreed that he is to be laid down without delay. At the usual hour this morning you will take the male into the wilderness and put him down in his original place of interment. Further, you will mark the burial place in an appropriate manner for future reference. *That* grave shall never again be opened and *that* male shall never again be recovered for service. He is permanently expelled as an enemy of the city."

Kehli said, "Wytha. . . ."

Wytha indicated the stack of newly minted caskets lining the side wall. Her index finger jabbed the air.

"Take a container with you. This meeting is closed."

Owen Hall blinked at the sudden finality of it and turned his head to look at his almost-patron.

"That's murder, Kelly."

Fourteen

The plain man is the basic clod
From which we grow the demigod;
And in the average man is curled
The hero stuff that rules the world.
                                    —Sam Walter Foss

Owen Hall's second day of his new life began with uncertainty, misdoubt. It was a second life, his second time around, and that contributed to the confusion. His second-day look at this new world convinced him it was not the promised land—not the Eden-like garden he had been led to expect. They had robbed him of that.

He had been tried and found wanting, discourteously. They weren't supposed to do that in Utopia.

The new sun hurt his eyes because he'd been used to the long hours of darkness inside Kehli's house, the hours before dawn that were lighted only by two candles. The sun was rising with the quick heat of summer, rising into a cloudless sky that surely promised hot and discomforting hours to come. He recognized it as an August sun, but it really shouldn't be summertime, shouldn't be the beginning of his second day. An August sun was out of place, as strange as the rolling roadway that now carried him, a prisoner, into the northeast. He was immobile.

His mind insisted that this should be wintertime and there should be ice and snow on the land. He held a clear

memory of deep snows everywhere on the prairie, of ice
on the highway, a vivid memory of a blizzard blowing
around him with snow or sleet stinging his face. He
should be in the harsh middle of an Indiana winter, not
here in the young morning hours of a summer day sur-
rounded by hostile shepherds who looked on him as a
hateful object. Owen stood in a line of five zombie workmen, securely bound to two of them while two others
carried his coffin. The fifth man bringing up the rear held
a blanket and a basket lunch.

There was a healthy stand of summer grass on the
lawns before the row houses and an enormous prairie of
grass that began just beyond the rolling road. The prairie
seemed to fill all of the new world from one horizon to
the other, occupying all of the visible world off the roadway. Lush turf was everywhere, as pastures and croplands had once been everywhere before the subdivisions
came; this was clean, green country unspoiled by highways, billboards, and hamburger houses—much as it had
been in his youth.

That part of the world could be the promised land.

In the far distance, off there to the east, a stand of timber grew against the horizon, fine trees standing tall before the sun. The day was already so bright that Owen
had to squint to see the timber. The grove was as inviting
as ever and again it would be pleasantly cool under
those trees—cool and inviting later in the day when the
sun scorched the town. A place for introspection. Next
to fishing, the woods were the best place for thinking
and dreaming—the place for living yesterday over again
and for plotting tomorrow before it came. He wanted to
visit the grove again, to loaf and talk to the friendly squirrel once more. Given the peacefulness of those woods
and the inspiration of unfettered freedom, he might eventually puzzle out the riddle of this new world.

It was definitely not the happy kingdom promised by
Pastor Coulson, as the pastor himself must surely know
by now, but it could be an offbeat version of the fiery
place that preachers often reserved for backsliders. That
gauzy golden land in the sky wasn't likely to have drab
row houses, moving roads predicted by magazine writ-
ers, and tall domineering females intent on his destruc-
tion. They encircled Owen and the dull-eyed workmen,

riding the road with him to the place of departure. None were smiling.

Owen Hall thought them a rum bunch.

The road was filling with men—males who behaved like sleepwalkers or dummies, males who displayed all the energy and animation of anemic zombies. They traveled singly or in pairs, but there was no fraternization between them, no gossiping of last night's conquest or defeat, no retelling of yesterday's baseball scores. No one spoke of Rogers Hornsby's lifetime record of 2,259 games, no one cracked a sniggering joke about Betty Grable's legs, no one of them talked to his fellow even though the fellow was alongside elbow to elbow, cheek by jowl. The workmen were models of inert bodies, rebuilt to serve their captors.

An old cemetery came into view. It was more than merely old, it was ancient—a place long abandoned to the wilderness. The marble monuments and the smaller stones had tumbled over in neglect, fallen to the vandals of time and wind, while weeds and tall grasses grew everywhere in an attempt to obliterate the few remaining traces of the stones. Bases and pedestals were already lost to the weeds and their presence had to be guessed at. Owen knew the cemetery lacked a decent fishing hole.

Kehli gave an order and the workmen left the road and jumped down into the weedy grass. Owen jumped with them because he had no other choice—either he jumped or he'd be dragged down head over heels when the two lead men quit the road. The bonds between them were taut.

The pair carrying the new coffin came down heavily behind Owen and, lastly, the fellow toting Kehli's lunch and the pink blanket. They assembled in single file on the path beaten between the city and the distant cemetery. Kehli spoke again and the troupe moved off.

Owen turned his head to look behind.

A full dozen wardens were lined up along the lawns on the inner side of the roadway to watch him go, Paoli amongst them. Their faces were hard and unfriendly. He would have blown a farewell kiss to Paoli if his hands had been free and would have thumbed his nose at the others. A pity none would know the meaning of the gesture.

Owen glanced at the coffin to make certain the zombies were handling it with the proper care and faced forward to study the nape of Kehli's neck. He thought it a lovely neck, one that invited caressing.

Persuading Kehli to use the coffin to carry a payload to the cemetery hadn't been as difficult as he'd expected. His two backpacks had been resting against the rear wall of her apartment when he was returned there under guard after the trial, and Owen counted that a blessing.

He'd said, "Kelly, I want to take these with me."

She looked from the sacks to Owen. "I do not understand."

"I have to take these to the graveyard tomorrow—I mean today. It's important."

"Are the artifacts meaningful to you?"

He nodded vigorously. "Cupcake, old ancient people like me wouldn't dream of going to the graveyard without them. It would rile my honorable ancestors."

Kehli hesitated, eyeing the rucksacks and then the shepherds standing guard at both doors. No one offered an objection, and she gave her consent. Owen had stored the supplies in the coffin, closed the lid, and stood by to await the arrival of the native bearers.

The prairie seemed empty of life other than for the plodding troupe—well, other than for Owen and Kehli. The workmen were suspect. There were no cattle visible, no livestock of any kind, and nary a sign of a plow. The sod of the prairie had not been turned for a small eternity to judge by the overgrowth on every side. Owen wondered again if he was looking at buffalo grass. His grandfather had told him that the prairies were once covered by buffalo grass before the sodbusters cut it up or burned it off to make room for their settlements.

"Kelly?"

The woman didn't answer.

"Kelly, I sure as shooting made people mad back there at the council meeting. What did I say wrong?"

She walked on for a length of time before answering. Her voice was low and Owen strained to hear.

"You voiced a grievous blasphemy in speaking of the Mother. You were disrespectful—you demanded to see her and speak to her."

"I just wanted to appeal to a higher court," Owen protested. "Doesn't she have the last word?"

"No one demands an audience with Mother—no one sees her unless she first consents to an audience. Males are not permitted in her presence and certainly may not speak to her or about her. You desecrated her name, Owen Hall."

"You and I talked about her yesterday right here on the trail."

"I regret that. If I had not spoken of her you would have no knowledge, and you would not be in this position."

He kept his gaze on the back of her neck. "I'm sorry about that, Kelly. I'm truly sorry and I apologize to you. I meant no disrespect to the lady—I was only trying to get justice."

Kehli's head was bowed. After a while she said, "I believe you, Owen Hall, and thank you for the apology. The matter cannot be undone now."

"Murder," Owen said again. "You've been ordered to commit murder. That upset you last night when we talked about the skull—that guy who was bushwhacked."

"I am very distressed. It has not happened before."

"Never in all your history—you said that at the supper table. Well, now civilization is coming to the city, cupcake." He stared at her neck and bowed head. "I have the honor of being the first man to be killed around here, and you have the honor of being the first killer. I don't think you're going to like it."

She made no answer.

"It'll be my second time," Owen mused. "I was killed the first time back there in Indiana, but not by a man or a woman. A train hit me."

The enormity of the prairie excited his sense of wonder a second time, just as the sight of it had done yesterday. A vast and unending sea of grass except for the timber and adjoining cemetery. Quite literally the grass stretched from one horizon to the other without a visible break—without a house, barn, silo, or gasoline station. The great prairie was empty of roads, rail trackage, billboards, or telegraph poles; it revealed neither humans, horses, cattle, barking dogs, or the furrows of a plow. There were no windmills. Thousands of lush empty acres filled the world to the farthest reaches of his sight, a world that Kehli and her kind called a wilderness. There were no junkyards. The whole world seemed empty but for the town behind him and the few people on the trail with him, and that enormous vacuity stirred his imagination.

They reached the ancient cemetery.

Kehli stopped and gave an order in a low voice. The workmen obediently halted and bunched up behind her, awaiting the next instructions. They may have followed this same routine every day for the past five or ten years, yet they wouldn't pick up a shovel and turn a load of dirt until they were told to do so.

Owen asked, "Which one was my grave?"

She glanced at him and then indicated an excavation several feet away, next beyond the pit he had entered to reclaim the topaz ring. It lacked a headstone.

"Somebody was kind of chintzy," he observed. "Unless, of course, the mice carried it away."

Kehli gave another order and the two workmen carrying the coffin placed it on the ground and picked up their shovels. The fifth man carried the lunch basket and the blanket to the tree line and then waited there in the shade because he hadn't been instructed to return. The first pair in line, stoutly roped to Owen, did nothing but look at Kehli's pink uniform.

She faced Owen with irresolution.

"Now?" he asked.

"It is supposed to be now."

"You'll need all your courage, Kelly. It ain't easy."

"I am deeply troubled by the thought, Owen Hall."

"You'll be more troubled by the act. How do you figure on doing it?"

She removed a short length of rope from her pocket.

Owen said, "Civilization had that too—we called it garroting. It won't be neat and easy cupcake. A man who is garroted kicks and struggles a lot, so take care I don't boot you in the stomach. Protect your stomach." He looked up into her unhappy face. "There's an easier and quicker way if you've got the guts for it."

The troubled woman only looked at him, unable to put her question into words.

"Open the coffin and look in my rucksacks there. You'll find a knife in one of the packs, a very good knife

with a blade maybe six inches long. It's quality stuff—
I made it myself."

He watched while Kehli obeyed his instructions but
was quickly surprised to see her go directly to the proper
pack and retrieve the better knife without having to
search for it. She turned and held it up for his inspection.

"That's the one, and you knew it was there. You've
already gone through my packs, cupcake." He pursed
his lips and nodded. "You didn't report all *that* to the
council, but you knew what I was going to do with it—
with them."

"I did not wish to increase your troubles, Owen Hall."

"Thank you again, cupcake. Bring the knife here."

Kehli approached him slowly and with apprehension.

"If my hands were free I'd show you where to stick it,"
Owen said. "Come closer, you've got to touch me. Now
put one finger on my ribs—here—and feel for the soft
spot in between the ribs." He looked down at her unwilling hand. "No, not *there*, you're too low. Bring your finger up higher. There, now you've got it. My heart is
there, Kehli." He looked up into her face and read the
despair in the soft brown eyes that had earlier captivated
him. "The technique is to lay the point of the knife in
that spot between my ribs and drive it in hard and fast
with the heel of your other hand. Hard and *fast*, Kelly.
That way, no kicking, no struggling, and you don't get
booted in the stomach, because I won't have time to feel
it."

She snatched her finger away and backed off.

"Why are you saying this? Why are you aiding me?"

"I'm trying to make it easier on me," Owen said hon-
estly, "and make it easier on you, too."

"I do *not* understand you again!"

"I said last night at the supper table that I was falling
in love, Kelly. Today I've done fell. I *am* in love and a
man in love does funny things. I'm trying to make this
easier for you. That knife is better than garroting."

The woman stood without moving in the hot summer
sun and stared at him, searching his face and his eyes for
any nuance or reservation not present in his words.

She said, "It is forbidden for a woman to form an
emotional attachment for a recovery, a male."

"It ain't forbidden for a male to form one for a female

—and if it *was*, I'd ignore that law too." He tried to wave his hands toward the distant town but only succeeded in yanking the rope tying him to the patient zombie ahead. "You know what I think of them and their rules. All that stuff is for the birds, cupcake. When you fall in love you're *in* love and there ain't nothing else you can do about it, rules or no rules. It's *done*."

She bent forward to peer into his eyes.

"My equilibrium is the same as yesterday, cupcake."

"I think you are speaking the truth, Owen Hall."

"I am. You can count on it."

"You are speaking the truth about an emotional attachment."

"That's what I meant. Skip the equilibrium."

After a long while she broke off her study of his face and looked away toward the town. The figures of wardens and workmen were small things, poorly seen at the distance.

She said, "There are two courses of action."

"Three."

"I know of—" She broke off her inspection of the distant town and turned back to Owen. "Three?"

He nodded. "Three. The first course is the one you've already considered. You can obey your instructions from the council and put me down with style; you can push that knife into my heart and seal me in that coffin and drop me into the same old hole that I came out of; you can toss in my rucksacks and cover it all up, and—*poof!* —like a magic wand, twenty-four hours are wiped out as if I'd never been. You can march back into town tonight and tell Wytha the deed is done. That's one choice.

"Second choice. The second choice is also one that you've considered, or at least had serious thoughts about ever since you opened my rucksacks and found what I had stored away for a rainy day. You guessed what I had in mind and the second choice is easier on both of us. Especially me. You can cut these ropes and set me free; you can let me gather up my packs and head for the wilderness yonder, a free man. I wouldn't cut and run from here where I might be seen. I'd drift over there to the timber where that guy is standing and sort of fade through the trees to the far side—and *then* I'd light out into the wilderness. You know I'll never come back to this town

—you know that you'll never be found out on account of me.

"If you make *that* choice you've already figured out how to cover your own tracks. Me, I'd do about the same thing. I'd fill that coffin with dirt and bury it in my old grave, and then I'd lay stones over the grave and leave a sign saying, 'Do not open until Christmas,' just like Wytha ordered. You can go back to town tonight and tell her the deed is done, chop-chop, and the council is happy and you're happy and I'm happy. Oh, *especially* I'm happy. That's the second choice, Kelly."

The troubled brown eyes studied him.

"The third alternative?"

Softly: "I'm surprised you didn't think of the third way out, cupcake. It's the very best one. You and me go together." He bent his head in a gesture toward the great green prairie. "Out there, the two of us together. You can sing and I'll fish."

She took a sudden step backward in surprise and then the fuller implications of his bold suggestion struck her. Kehli's lips opened to reject the startling proposal out of hand, but no sound was heard. The hand holding his knife moved and flapped in an unconscious motion, betraying her amazement.

"Don't say no until you've heard me out, Kelly. I want the third choice—I want you to go with me. Please give it very careful thought."

The woman stared, wide-eyed.

"We could cover our tracks in just about the same way as before, only more so. See that poor stiff standing over there in the shade?" Owen motioned with his fingers. "He can't be seen from the town—he's covered by the timber. But he won't come back out here in the sun until you tell him to—he can't do anything until you tell him to do it. That guy will be our decoy in case anybody is looking. Cut me loose from these zombies and walk me over to the trees where that man is standing. Walk slow. Stall there for a minute or so and then walk back out with *him*. I'll stay hidden in the timber.

"When you're out here in plain sight, right by the crew and the coffin, put your hands around the man's neck and tell him to flop down in the grass and stay there a while. Don't hurt him! Lordy, lordy, Kelly, don't hurt the poor guy—just make him lie down and play dead.

"Fill my coffin with dirt and bury it just like before. Get my rucksacks out of it first, though, and smuggle them into the trees, but have this here crew put down the coffin and cover the grave with stones. Leave your message on it like Granny said. No matter what happens later, the folks in town will think you did your duty and I'm safely buried there—good riddance. After that you can relax—take a nip, if you like. I brought some with me.

"Put the crew to work filling in an empty grave—give them something to do to keep them busy until sundown —and instruct that guy loafing on the grass to grab a shovel and sneak back into the action so he can be just one of the boys at quitting time. Now, you—Kelly, you should drift over to the timber like you're going to take a nap or sample your picnic lunch. Presto!"

"Owen Hall, you are as mad as the ancient ones!"

"Sometimes I'm madder, cupcake—I've got a second chance working for me here, but they never had that. Hear me out. When you drift over into the shade, we'll grab the backpacks and skedaddle into the tall timber. That means run like hell. There's two packs—one for you and one for me. We can travel faster that way and by sundown we'll be long gone hunting the buffalo. The wilderness is ours, all ours, to explore, and you can sing your heart out if you want. I'll clap my hands and keep time."

"This is absurd! Wytha will come here for an inspection."

"Of course she will. Scared or not, that gutsy old granny will come tearing out here to see what happened to you. *You*, Kelly. I don't think she'll come out tonight, not after dark, even with a dozen cops and torches to ward off the ghosts and dragons. Those women are scared of the graveyard and scared of the wilderness. Granny will come out here first thing tomorrow at the crack of dawn—and she'll find my grave but no trace of you. We'll be over the hills and far away by sunrise."

"Wytha will see—"

"She'll see the new grave, as ordered, and she'll see your blanket and the picnic basket—an empty picnic basket, which will make her think you were still here at noontime. She'll even search the timber."

Kehli parted her lips to speak again, but her vocal chords were uncooperative. The rising sun limned her rich brown hair and caused her to squint against the brightness. Owen's knife hung limp in her hand.

"You're trying to think of more objections," Owen said. "Don't bother. I know how to cover trail and how to leave no trail at all. I know how to use creeks and rocky ground to travel for miles without a trail. I ain't no Kit Carson, but I know twice as much about the outside world as those dames in town. The big point is, you and me ain't afraid of the prairie but they are.

"I want to show you the pretty country, Kelly. I want to show you what we've got two or three hundred miles south of here. There's a little canyon and a waterfall at an ol' place called Turkey Run that'll take your breath away. There's hill country farther south like you've never seen in all your born days. And the Ohio—just wait until you *see* that river! Over on the Illinois side there's a place called Cave-in-Rock, where pirates used to hide and then jump out on the river traffic. Hoo boy, Kelly, I want to show you everything!"

Kehli found her voice. "I must choose—" She was unable to complete the sentence.

Owen Hall nodded. "You've got to do the choosing. All I can do right now is stand here and wait. The sun's getting kinda hot out here and this zombie didn't have a bath."

Kehli was painfully aware of her dilemma.

She gazed back toward the distant town as if seeking a solution to the dilemma but found nothing other than the tiny figures of workmen and shepherds on the road. Their ranks were thinning out as the males left the roadway and reported for work, while shepherds were even fewer in number. Her watchful audience had gone. Close at hand a solitary male waited in the cool shade of the forest for his next command. The pink blanket and her lunch basket hung on his arm.

Immediately before her were the four males who comprised the remainder of the work party and the man she had been told to put down. He waited for her decision, trussed between two of the workmen but patiently watching her face. Kehli was uncomfortable under his unwavering gaze. She raised her hand to study the new shiny knife taken from the rucksack and knew that the point of the blade was cruelly sharp. She could not bring herself to look up at the man for long moments.

"Some folks call that a widow-maker," Owen Hall said. "Use it smartly, or put it away."

Fifteen

Here with a little Bread beneath the Bough,
A Flask of Wine, a Book of Verse—and Thou
——Beside me singing in the Wilderness—
Oh, Wilderness were Paradise enow!
　　　　　　　—Omar Khayyam
　　　　　　　(FitzGerald's second edition)

Owen Hall trod carefully, smelling the nearness of water and knowing what was to come. The undergrowth was heavy and treacherous, unlike that first easy timber he'd found outside the city, and he took care not to misstep. To trip over his own feet and fall headfirst down the scarp would be a damned-fool thing to do. The trees were thinning and he knew he was approaching the brink.

He moved on slowly, placing each foot firmly on the ground before him to test the earth and clinging to each tree for support in case the ground should suddenly drop away from under him. The brink had to be close.

Owen stopped suddenly, took a step back to firmer ground, and stared through the trees to the vista below.

The river was thirty-five or forty feet below him at the bottom of a weedy embankment. He was standing at the very edge of the scarp looking down on the flowing water, so near that he could spit into the shallows of the near shore. Owen thought he saw deer prints in the mud of the shore. The heavy timber grew around him for miles in either direction, upriver and down, and he would not have found the river so easily if it had not been for the westerlies carrying the smell of water. He knew he was somewhere in southwestern Indiana and knew the river had to be there unless the pink ladies had stolen it, but he had relied on the west wind to help him find it.

Kehli came up behind him, thrashing and stumbling through the thick underbrush. He put out a quick hand to stop her and save her from tumbling over the edge. She caught her breath and stared downward with great round eyes.

"What *is* it, Owen Hall?"

"That's the ol' Wabash, Kelly. Ain't it a beauty?"

"What is a wabash?"

"The Wabash River, tourist! I've been waiting three weeks to see that sight—several hundred years and three weeks." He looked around at Kehli. "I think we've been gone from the old home town about three weeks. Now, ain't that a *real* beauty? It would be romantic if we had some moonlight."

The woman stayed transfixed by the spectacle. "What does one do with a wabash river?"

Owen Hall laughed aloud and would have clapped his hands if he dared let go both supporting trees.

"One fishes in it, cupcake. One takes a bath in it every Saturday night, one swims in it, cooks with it, and drinks it—but not all at the same time in the same place if you want to stay sanitary. With a little work, one can even lash together a raft and float downriver on it, and we just might do that, because the Ohio is down there somewhere—down south, yonder." He relaxed his hold on one of the trees and reached out for Kehli's hand. "Would you like to go down and sing in it? I'll bet you never sang in a river before."

"I have not seen a river before."

"Bully!" Owen Hall said. "This is going to be another historic first, like Lindbergh crossing the Atlantic on one engine. Let's work our way down and stick a toe in the water. And tonight, if I can remember all the words, I'll teach you how to sing "Moonlight on the Wabash." My grandmother used to sing that all the time. Now, there was a spry old gal."

The palmy days had begun.